The House on Dragonfly Lane

Kay J. Cee

Table *of* Contents

This is the story of the little house on Dragonfly Lane. Small and unassuming, it played a part in so many lives throughout the years.

You could easily miss the turn off to Dragonfly Lane. It was a one lane, gravel road, if you could call it that. It was more a gravel path with a strip of grass down the middle of it. Large trees bordered the road and allowed the sunshine to peek through occasionally. The path took so many twists and turns through the woods, just as you thought you had reached the end, it veered off in another direction.

There was only the one house on Dragonfly Lane. It was a tiny red brick cottage with black shutters and a forest green door. Ivy grew along the house walls. It was virtually hidden from the world and seemed a part of the forest itself. Large paned windows opened out onto a yard with little grass, but full of clover and wildflowers. A chimney stood in the center of the red tiled roof.

There were only four rooms in the whole cottage and they formed a square. A small living room with large windows looked out onto the yard. The fireplace was a wood stove, black, with glass so you could enjoy the flickering flames. There was a bathroom with white penny tiles along the floor and walls. A tiny sink hung off the wall with a medicine chest and mirror above it. The rest of the room was taken up by a claw foot tub, gleaming white with gold feet.

The next door led around to the bedroom. It too had large paned windows, which opened out onto a tiny overgrown garden in the back. The last room was the kitchen. Its space was almost completely taken up with a white porcelain stove. It was as old as the house, but looked showroom new. There were very few cabinets and those ran along the lower half. The top half had open shelving, but even that was limited. The sink was a tiny farmhouse one, barely able to fit the dishes from one meal. The refrigerator was the only nod to modernism. Thankfully it was not an icebox. The table folded up and latched to the wall when not in use.

A door in the wall by the table, opened up onto a patio paved with worn flagstones. Sprigs of grass grew up between them. What should have looked unkempt, instead looked green, lush, and welcoming. It made you want to take off your shoes and feel the cool of the stones and the tickle of thick grass on your feet.

Mr. Charles O'Shaunessy, the owner of the cottage, was a small round man with an unrecognizable accent. His name would suggest Irish or Scottish, but it was impossible to pinpoint either one. He had graying hair, almost silver and green eyes that twinkled when he smiled. He smiled all the time, and his grin spread wide across his face.

He dressed in a suit, a little old fashioned, complete with bow tie. He carried a bowler hat, black, and a cane that seemed to be just for show as he walked with a spring in his step. His look was completed with a pair of round glasses. His age was hard to determine, as his spryness and quick pace belied any passage of years.

Tilly and Sam

The 1940s

Tilly worked at Willoughby Drug Store on the corner of Second and Franklin Street. She made milk shakes and cherry cokes at the soda fountain for all the teens that came on Friday nights after the football game. The football games she never got to go to. But Tilly didn't mind, her family didn't have much money and what she brought home was needed to get by. She was sixteen years old and the oldest of eight children.

Five days a week, Tilly stood behind the counter. Every day was the same. No one paid much attention to her, except to bark out drink orders and she was used to that. Never engaging in conversation and just answering with a smile, had earned her the nickname, 'Mona Lisa".

Until Friday night when he walked in. She was used to young soldiers coming in, after all, Camp Campbell was just north of town. They would often compliment her or tease her, anything to get her attention. She ignored them. When the young soldier with a crew cut and a book in his hand walked in, she took no special notice. Until he came back the next week and the next.

He sat in the back-corner booth, with his head down, reading a book, one of the classics. He always ordered a plain hamburger and a coke. He never came up to the counter, so Tilly was only mildly curious because of his predictability.

That Friday, the young soldier came in and all the booths were taken by the football team and their cheerleader dates. They had won the local championship game and were being loud and rowdy. The soldier managed to find a stool at the counter, sat down, and opened his book.

The football players were hopped up on their win and some became obnoxious. One of them reached out and took hold of the bow tied back of Tilly's apron. She grabbed the front of it to keep it from slipping but dropped the tray of cokes she held. Tilly's cheeks burned red as the players and their dates laughed at her expense. She turned quickly to get a mop, but another player stuck out his foot and tripped her. As she tried to steady herself, she felt a strong arm reach around to hold her. It was the soldier who had come to her rescue. After he got her back behind the counter, he turned to the player who had gotten to his feet. The soldier walked over, his back ramrod straight, and looked down at the burly lineman.

"Isn't there something you want to say to the lady? Or rather, something you need to say?"

The lineman stuck out his chest and pushed back at the soldier. "What business is it of yours doggie? Don't you have a war to be fought somewhere?"

The soldier reached out with a balled right fist and punched the boy dead in the eye. Everyone gasped. The football players grabbed their girlfriends and the boy and sheepishly walked out the front door.

Tilly stood behind the counter, speechless. No one had ever stood up for her before and she didn't know what to say.

The soldier walked over, stuck out his hand and introduced himself. "Hello, my name is Sam and I'm sorry those jerks bothered you. Are you okay?" His deep green eyes looked deeply into hers.

Tilly stared back into those eyes and shook her head to get her mind back on what he had said. "Oh yes, I'm okay. Those boys think they run the whole town, especially when they win a big game. Thank you for coming to my rescue."

"It was my pleasure, miss," he said with a smile and a slight southern drawl.

The night finished out uneventfully, especially since Sam stayed around until closing to make sure. He offered to walk Tilly to the bus stop. He kept a respectful distance, and didn't try to make a pass. She was grateful for that after a night like tonight.

After that, Sam showed up every night, and sat in the corner booth reading. After a week, Tilly traded jobs with another girl and began waiting on him herself. It started with shy smiles and always ended with a walk to the bus stop.

One Friday night, Sam asked Tilly if he could call on her that next night. Tilly froze, unsure what to say. It wasn't that she was embarrassed by her house, after all, it was all they could afford. But looking at it through his eyes, she could just imagine what he would think.

What shutters they had, hung on for dear life by their broken hinges. Broken panes of glass were covered with pieces of cardboard, on which her younger sister had drawn pictures on. The stairs leaned one step to one side, one to the other. You took your life in your hands to even try to climb them. The house was, at least, six different colors. The kids had painted it with whatever color they could find. This was all before you got in the front door.

Inside was a mismatch ensemble of whatever could be found on the side of the road and patched up. The floor was a painted piece of oilcloth, so worn that the pattern could no longer be seen.

A single light bulb hung by a string in the center of the room, casting eerie shadows along the bare walls.

Tilly thought fast, "I have chores to do around the house. Why don't you meet me at the drug store around five?"

Sam, happy to get a somewhat affirmative answer, agreed quickly. "How about a movie? *Buck Privates* is showing at the Capitol. Abbott and Costello are always funny."

Tilly nodded quickly. She didn't want to seem too eager. It wasn't like the last time she went to the movies was over three years ago.

And so, it became a weekly ritual. Sam at the drug store during the week. Movies on the weekends or long walks down along the river.

After a few weeks of this, Sam insisted on taking her home. He declared it was past a respectful time to meet her parents, and he needed to correct that right away.

"Oh, they're probably busy putting kids to bed. We can wait for another night," Tilly tried to reason.

"No, I won't stay long. I just feel that it's disrespectful to you and your parents not to introduce myself."

What could Tilly say? "Okay, I understand. But let's just make it a short visit, okay?"

Tilly flinched when they turned the corner of Marion Street and her house came into view. She could only pray that the details would be blurred a little by the fading twilight. Her hand trembled a little from nerves. She prayed her brothers and sisters were already in bed.

She led him up the wonky steps. She stopped him before they went through the door. "Um, let me just explain that Papa's been out of work for a while now, so things are in a little bit of disrepair right now. He and Mama do the best they can," she said as she slowly pushed open the door. She didn't dare look up at Sam's face, afraid to see any look of pity or disgust he might exhibit.

Sam's presence filled the small, front room. Papa walked in from the kitchen. "Ma, looks like we have company."

Mama came in, wiping her hands on her apron. "Well, mercy me, Tilly. Who is this you've brought home?"

Sam put out his right hand and grasped Papa's hand in a firm handshake. He nodded his head politely toward Mama. "My name is Sam Elliot, sir, ma'am."

"Well, have a seat, son, and tell us a little about yourself."

Tilly held her breath as Sam took a seat in the ricketiest chair in the house and prayed it didn't break from this weight. She glanced over at Mama and noticed she too was holding her breath. Papa and Sam paid them no mind and continued with their conversation.

"Sir, I am an infantry soldier stationed at Camp Campbell. This is my first year stationed here and I'll be moving out as soon as our new orders come through."

Tilly's head whipped around, and her eyes grew large. This was the first she had heard him speak of any future plans. Most of their conversations centered around hometowns, family, and dreams of the future. She never considered he might have to go away. She quit worrying about the chair breaking or even her siblings peeking through the doorway and stayed tuned into Sam and Papa's conversation.

They were engrossed in the whys and wheres of the current military efforts and paid little attention to the women. Mama interrupted, "How long have you and our Tilly been seeing each other now?"

"About five weeks now ma'am," Sam answered before Tilly could.

"And this is the first time we've met you, let alone even heard your name mentioned. Tilly, shame on you," her mother admonished her. "Well, now that we've met, Sam, don't you be a stranger here."

Tilly blushed. Sometimes her parents could embarrass the life out of her.

Sam smiled, "Ma'am, I sure appreciate that."

"Why, you should come to lunch tomorrow. I'm sure it's been quite a while since you've had a home cooked meal," her mother said. "It won't be anything fancy but it will be filling."

"Mama!" Tilly exclaimed. "He might have other plans. Sam, don't feel like you have to accept if you have something else to do."

"I'd love a home cooked meal, ma'am. I'd be mighty pleased to accept your kind invitation," Sam said with a smile toward Tilly.

After what seemed like an eternity of questions, Sam got up to leave. Tilly walked him to the door amidst calls of 'see you tomorrow, son' and 'lunch is around one o'clock, but you come on early'.

She was too embarrassed to give him even a tiny peck on the cheek, not knowing how many of her brothers and sisters were peeking out the window. She settled with an awkward hand shake. How silly was that? He gave her a quick smile and nodded at one of the windows where you could see two little faces looking on. And with that he went off down the street whistling.

Tilly got up early Sunday morning, well before anyone else, and started to clean and straighten up. She did the best she could but felt like it was putting lipstick on a pig. Now, she wasn't ungrateful for all her mama and papa had done for the family. But it was the first time she had looked at the house from someone else's point of view and she found it seriously lacking.

By the time everyone had eaten breakfast and gotten dressed, Tilly had spruced up the little house as best she could.

Tilly corralled everyone together after church and got them home as quickly as possible. Her mama started cooking while Tilly admonished the little ones to stay decently clean because they were having company.

Sam arrived promptly at one and papa got to the door first. They both sat down on the front porch and Tilly could barely hear what they were talking about through the old screen window.

"You let those menfolk have their talk now and you get the table set," her mama told her. "Use the good dishes." Those consisted of mismatched pieces of discarded china that papa had managed to salvage from the trash pile down the street. But the flowers Tilly had picked and placed in an old glass, made the table look fairly pretty.

Lunch was a fun, rowdy affair. The kids asked Sam all kinds of questions about the Army. The oldest boy wanted to know what it was like to shoot a gun. While the youngest was more interested if the food was any good. All the kids were thrilled to hear tales about where he grew up and the old fort that was on an island in the ocean.

Mama asked a lot of questions about his home and family. Sam explained that both his parents had died when he was ten and he was raised by this aunt and uncle in Charleston. Sam explained that the lack of a permanent sense of home, played a large part of his decision to join the military.

Papa stayed quiet, though Tilly did catch him watching her a few times during the meal. After the meal, mama told her and Sam to go on out to the porch and cool off while she and papa cleaned up the dishes. Tilly had never in all her life known papa to help with the dishes and she wondered what that was all about.

Sam pulled the two chairs closer together and as out of sight of the front door as possible. They sat there in silence for a few minutes then he reached out and took her hand in his. He looked deep into her eyes and Tilly felt a flutter in her stomach. What was going on?

"Tilly, I got my orders this week. I'll be shipping out in two weeks. They've not told us where we're going and I have no idea how long I will be gone."

Her face fell and she grasped his hand tighter.

"I had not planned on doing this so soon, please forgive me for my haste. Tilly, I can't offer you much except my love, but would you do the honor of marrying me?" he stammered. "I have asked your father, and he gave his permission."

Tilly began to cry. "Oh yes! I would be proud to be your wife, Sam."

They both stood and Sam grabbed Tilly by the waist and spun her around the porch. The screen door creaked open and papa said, "Well, I guess you and your mama will need to plan a wedding now." And he shook Sam's hand.

Everyone went inside where mama hugged Sam's neck and kissed Tilly. "Let's get started. We don't have much time to get you two married," she said with a smile.

With such a short time before Sam left, it was decided to get married at the courthouse. None of Tilly's dresses were special enough, so they took one of her mama's and cut it down to fit. One of her mama's hats would do nicely with a little sandpaper to make it look as new as possible. Tilly would make her bouquet out of the wildflowers in the little back garden.

A week later, their wedding day dawned clear and bright without a cloud in the sky. Sam looked so handsome in his uniform. He stood with his back ramrod straight and a solemn look on his face. Tilly's cheeks had a natural blush. She looked so tiny and fragile in her mama's dress. It didn't take ten minutes for the judge to declare them husband and wife. After a small reception at Tilly's house, Sam pulled his bride aside and whispered that he had a surprise for her. They hugged everyone goodbye and left to begin their life together.

Sam had borrowed a buddy's car and they drove a few streets over until they came to a small overgrown path. Sam turned down it. The trees on the side of the path seemed to form a canopy enclosing the couple into their own magical place. At the end of the winding path stood a small red brick cottage covered in ivy. A green front door was bordered on either side with large pane windows.

Tilly gasped and grabbed Sam's hand and asked "What is this Sam? Are we staying here for the night? Does it belong to one of your friends?"

Sam turned to her with a grin and said "No, this is all ours for as long as we want to stay here."

"How did you ever find it, Sam? It is the perfect place to start our lives together!"

"Well, that is quite a story. When I waited for you outside the drugstore last week, this man came up to me and asked if I knew where he could post a house for rent. I asked him a few questions and the next day we rode out to look at it. I knew the minute I saw it that it would be perfect for us. It was like it was meant to be." Sam beamed with delight.

Tilly's eyes welled up with tears as a big smile broke across her face. She leaned over and gave Sam a big kiss. "Oh, Sam. I have never seen anything so beautiful in my whole life. It's all ours? For as long as we want?" She jumped out of the car before Sam could get it fully stopped.

"Hey, wait a minute. It's not going anywhere. You can't just go in. Remember, I get to carry you over the threshold." And with that, he swept Tilly up in his arms, opened the door, and went in.

The little cottage was furnished sparingly, but to Tilly, it looked like a mansion. There was a tiny wood stove in the center of the first room. There was also a small floral covered sofa and a few straight back chairs. Tilly ran to the next room, the kitchen. There was a cook stove in there and a tiny sink. Next was an indoor bathroom. Even a tiny sink clung to the wall. What luxury! Tilly was so excited.

She ran to the last room and stopped in her tracks. She turned to Sam with a blush as she saw the bed pushed up against the wall. He chuckled, took her hand, and led her back out to the first room. "What do you think, honey? Do you like it?"

Tilly threw her arms around his neck and buried her face in his chest. He could barely hear her say "It's perfect."

The next week passed in a blur as Sam spent much of his time at the base preparing to leave. However, at night, he would return to the little red brick cottage and the arms of his one true love.

The time came for Sam to leave and Tilly's heart was broken. It wasn't fair. Their time together had been so short. Why would God send such a good man into her life, only to separate them so quickly? All Tilly could do was pray that the war would end quickly and he would return safely to her.

Tilly kept busy working at the drug store. Every time a soldier came in, her heart would stop. Her mind would tell her it wasn't Sam, but her heart always hoped. She never got used to the disappointment.

She used the little money she earned to buy things for their little house to turn it into a home. With the war, things were scarce and many things were rationed, yet Tilly managed to make the cottage a welcoming place. She turned the flour sacks she took home from the store into curtains for the windows. She traded some of her ration tickets for furniture. Her favorite trade was a big cozy chair for Sam.

The town was full of blue-star flags to show how many of their family were servicemen. Tilly wanted to show her pride in Sam's service. She proudly placed a blue-star flag in the window, even though the flag couldn't be seen from the road.

All this kept her hands busy, but her mind constantly thought of Sam. She prayed as her hands worked the sewing needle and as she tended her little victory garden out back. Everything she did was in preparation for Sam's return.

She lived for late afternoon when the postman would leave mail at the end of the long road. Her feet fairly danced down the lane in anticipation of getting a letter from Sam. At first the letters were plentiful. Sam filled them with tales from camp and descriptions of people he met. The end of each letter contained many lines describing his adoration and love. Tilly kept each letter in a box by the bed tied together with the ribbon from her wedding flowers. She would pull them out each night and re-read them. Strangely, it made her feel as if Sam was right there with her.

As the months went by, the letters became fewer and shorter. There was still the declaration of love at the end, but Tilly sensed a change. In June, Tilly heard on the radio of the invasion of Normandy. She did not know what division Sam was in, but her gut feeling told her he was involved in this somehow and she was terrified. She devoured any news she could find. She read of the casualties and cried. Every walk down the lane to check for a letter was accompanied with a fervent prayer for Sam and all the men's safety. To return home without a letter was devasting.

Tilly tried hard to stay positive but it was difficult. People all around town got letters from their loved ones eventually. The unfortunate ones got visits from Western Union with news of missing in action, wounded, or killed in combat. It had been weeks now and she still had not heard a word.

One day in late June, Tilly heard a car drive up the lane. Her heart froze in fear. No one she knew even owned a car so she knew. She just knew. There were two sharp knocks on the door and she slowly rose. Her feet felt like lead as she dragged herself to the door. Glancing out the window, she saw the specially marked car that everyone in the country dreaded. She opened the door slowly and held onto the doorframe for support. The man looked sad as he handed her the telegram. She was afraid to touch it, afraid to open it. She knew that this envelope would change her life in some way or another. She closed the door without a word and sank down in Sam's chair, hoping to feel his comfort around her.

Slowly, Tilly slit open the envelope and pulled out the short message typed in long strips and pasted onto the sheet of paper. "We regret to inform you that Sam Elliot has", Tilly was crying so hard that she couldn't make out the rest of the words. Asking God for strength, she blinked hard, cleared the tears, and finished reading. "been reported missing in action". She didn't know how to react, so she continued crying. She cried in relief that he had not been reported killed. Then she cried because he was missing. Could he have been captured? Was he right now sitting in a prisoner of war camp? Was he hurt? So many unanswered questions. Her head spun.

Tilly took her Bible off the table and held it tight to her chest. She didn't know what to pray so she just repeated 'please God' over and over. It grew dark and Tilly, completely exhausted and still clutching the Bible, fell asleep in Sam's chair.

The next morning, Tilly walked the blocks to her parents' house. Her mama could tell with one look that something awful had happened. She began to whisper a prayer under her breath. Tilly held out the crumpled telegram and her mama carefully took it, smoothed out the paper, and read the dreaded words. Without a sound, she opened her arms and Tilly fell into them with a cry.

When Tilly's papa arrived home from the store, he knew without asking something had happened. He picked up the telegram and read it quickly. "You must come back home and stay with us, Tilly. You need your family now. I'll go with you to get your things."

Tilly shook her head. "No, sir. Thank you, but I can't."

"Then I will come over and stay with you. You don't need to be alone with this Tilly. I'll go pack up my things. Mrs. Thompson's oldest girl can come over and help out around the house for a while. It will be fine," mama said.

Tilly shook her head again. "No, ma'am. Thank you both but I need to be at the house. I feel closest to Sam there. I need to be there when he comes home. And I won't be alone, God is with both me and Sam."

Tilly left right before the smaller kids came home. She didn't want them to see her so upset. Her mama insisted and sent her home with supper even though she had no appetite. She walked up the lane as it grew dark and the fireflies came out. She took a moment to take in their beauty and it lightened her heart a little.

Evidence of God was everywhere and she knew He was with Sam wherever he was right now.

Months passed with no news. Tilly worked hard to keep her faith strong but as each day passed, her resolve weakened. Her attempts to get any further information were met with apologies, excuses, and no new word of Sam's whereabouts.

Tilly quit walking down the lane to check the mail. The postman knew the situation as did most people in town and if anything of any importance arrived, he delivered it to her door. Otherwise, she would walk down once a week and pick up anything he had left.

When Tilly saw the postman coming down the drive, she drew in a quick breath. The postman came to the door and called out her name. Tilly ran to open it and he excitedly pushed an envelope into her hands. "Tilly, Tilly, it's a letter from overseas. It's from Sam!"

Tilly hurriedly looked it over. It was from Sam, but not his handwriting. She thanked the postman and cautiously opened the envelope. Was this a letter that had been lost before the battle and now finally delivered or was it one that Sam had written recently? She told herself to be prepared no matter what.

The letter was also not in Sam's handwriting. It began with the explanation that it was written by a nurse in the hospital where Sam was recuperating. She wrote it exactly as he dictated it and she hoped it would encourage her.

"My darling Tilly, words cannot express how much I miss you. I pray God is looking after you and keeping you safe. I know you have been terribly worried and I am so sorry for that. I wish I could have let you know I was okay and they were taking good care of me here, but circumstances prevented that. I have been unconscious since they brought me in and it is only recently that I woke up. I am still having trouble using my right arm and leg though they are working with me on it. That is why I had someone else write this to you. I don't say this to worry you, as I feel I am stronger every day. The doctors say I may be shipped stateside as soon as it is safe for me to travel. I will be sure to keep you informed and perhaps you can come visit me if it is close by. I long to see your beautiful face and look into your beautiful eyes once again. Even with my difficulties, I consider myself blessed as many of my friends did not make it out of the battle. One day, I hope to tell you of the many heroes I have met along my journey. I miss you my darling and I long for the day I am with you once again. All my love, Sam."

Tears fell from Tilly's eyes as she read his letter over and over. He is alive! He is coming home! Thank you, Lord, was all she could say.

Tilly ran down the lane to her parents' house. She couldn't wait to give them the news. She burst in the house right as they were sitting down to supper. She waved the letter around and the smile on her face spoke volumes.

"He's okay! He's in a hospital, he couldn't say where. But he's okay," Tilly shouted joyfully.

Everyone began talking at once. Tilly held her hands up and beckoned for everyone to sit back down at the table. "Ya'll eat and I'll tell you what he said."

Her mama fixed her a plate, but she was too excited to take a bite. She read the letter out loud to everyone, omitting the personal parts meant just for her. Papa led them all in a prayer for

Sam's safe and quick return. Tilly stayed the night as her emotions had worn her out and she was too tired to walk all the way home.

The months crawled by with only the sporadic letter from Sam and never in his own handwriting. Tilly wasn't sure what was going on, but he assured her he was better each day and would soon be headed stateside.

The day finally came when Sam boarded a ship and headed home to the states and Tilly rejoiced over the news. He went to an Army hospital in San Francisco for rehabilitation on his right side. Sam assured her that everything was fine and he would be okay after this was finished.

San Francisco was too far for Tilly to visit so they had to depend on their weekly letters. After a couple of months, she received a letter with her address scrawled across the front. When she opened it, she realized that this letter Sam had written himself. His pride in his accomplishment came through each line and Tilly couldn't help but smile. He told her he should be discharged the next month as the doctor decided he could do the rest of his rehabilitation at the base hospital closer to home.

Tilly began sprucing up the little home. She polished every surface and plumped up all the pillows. She tilled and planted new flowers and vegetables in the victory garden. Closer to his return she used all her ration stamps to stock the ice box. People brought by cakes and pies, using their own sugar and flour ration stamps to welcome the hero home.

The day came when a car from the base pulled up in front of the house. Tilly ran to the door and tore it open. She ran outside and threw herself on Sam before he could even get fully out of the car.

Sam stumbled and grabbed hold of the door frame with his left hand and leaned on the car. Tilly saw that the driver of the car was looking on and took a quick step back, embarrassed at her show of enthusiasm. She wiped her hands on her apron and looked up at Sam. She noticed how he quickly hid a look of pain on his face and replaced it with a big smile. The driver got out and took Sam's duffle bag to the door. He then turned and saluted, climbed back in the car, and drove off.

Sam waited until he had pulled out of sight then wrapped his left arm around Tilly and gave her a big hug. He then leaned forward, looked deep into her eyes, and gave her a soft kiss. Tilly wrapped her arms around him and leaned her head on his chest. He was home, home at last. And she said a quick prayer of thanks for his return.

The couple took a few days to get accustomed to each other again. Sam set up his appointments at the hospital. He would need ongoing treatment to regain better use of his right arm and leg. All Tilly cared was that he was home.

After this, they went over to Tilly's parents for a big homecoming celebration. Tilly had warned everyone about his injuries and no one, not even the kids, said a word about them. After the meal, Tilly could hear Sam and her papa talking in the parlor. They discussed what Sam could do after he got better. Jobs were pretty scarce around here now, with so many servicemen returning home. Sam said a lot of his buddies were taking advantage of the opportunity to go to college and he would like to do that. He had always wanted to be a teacher but never had the chance to go to college. This was the first Tilly had heard of that and she thought it was a fine idea and planned to encourage him when he next brought the subject up.

The only thing that worried Tilly was that Sam had bad dreams. He would wake up sweating and crying out for everybody to get down. Sam went to therapy and the doctor said this was shell shock and hopefully it would ease up with time. Sam helped Tilly around the house, but mostly worked in the garden. It seemed to give his leg and arm a good workout. It also eased his mind as the dreams became less and less frequent. Their little garden had never looked better and Sam was regaining some use of his arm.

The next year, Sam signed up for classes at the college. He went for his teaching degree and Tilly couldn't have felt prouder. She would clean up after supper while Sam worked on his homework. The days flew by in the cozy little cottage, and the couple had never been happier.

In those days, the sun seemed to shine a little brighter over the cottage. Once Sam got his degree, he got a job teaching at the local high school. He was asked to teach English and he couldn't have been happier. Tilly started to work part-time at Parks Belk's department store to keep her busy. She loved interacting with the customers and helped them pick out what they needed.

One day late in the school year, another teacher rushed into Sam's school room. Tilly had fainted at work and she was calling for him. Sam rushed out and ran to the store. Tilly was sitting in a chair and her face was a ghostly shade of white. He grabbed her purse and helped her out to the manager's car. He drove as fast as he dared to the doctor's house. There, the doctor examined her and ran some tests. He told her to go home and rest until they heard back from him.

Tilly stayed in bed for the week and Sam waited on her hand and foot. She told him she felt much better but Sam refused to let her do anything. Finally, there was a knock on the door. Sam opened it to a smiling doctor. Sam was a little perturbed that he stood there smiling when Tilly had been so ill. He invited him in and they both went into the bedroom where Tilly laid. The doctor told Sam to sit down beside her and take her hand. They were both very nervous.

The doctor smiled at them both. "I am happy to announce that you two are going to have a baby. That is why Tilly fainted. She will be perfectly fine. I have brought her some vitamins to start taking. She is perfectly healthy and I see no reason that she won't have a perfectly healthy baby."

Sam jumped up with a whoop and a holler then remembered and leaned down and kissed Tilly right on the lips in front of the doctor. Tilly blushed but Sam wasn't sure if it was from happiness or embarrassment. He assumed both.

After the doctor left, Sam and Tilly sat down around the table and began to make plans. Sam's concern was how to fit another person into the little cottage. It would be fine while the baby was small and in a crib. But they would need more room as he grew. Sam broke the news to Tilly that they would probably need to leave the little brick cottage. Tilly grew sad. She loved their home and hated to leave it even for such a happy reason. The cottage had been her safe cocoon while Sam was away. It had caught all her tears when he went missing. The little garden had helped heal Sam in body and soul. It would hurt so bad to leave.

Sam could sense her hesitation. "I promise you, I will find us another house just as cozy as this one and together the three of us will make it a fine home. It will be a house that we can raise our children in and grow old together."

Tilly raised her head, tears shining in her eyes. "Our children? Why Sam, let's have this one first before we go talking about anymore. But you're right. I love this place, but home is wherever you are. Now let's go tell my papa that he's going to be a grandfather. He's going to burst with pride!"

Susan

The 1950s

Donald and Susan lived a typical fifties-era life. Maybe a little above average, but they tried not to be too showy about it. They had a two-story house with four bedrooms, two bathrooms, kitchen, formal dining room, living room, and den. The kitchen was outfitted with the latest gadgets and appliances. They even had a two-car garage and an inground pool which was the envy of all the neighbors.

Susan was head of the Relief Society at her church. Many functions were held at her lovely home and the ladies felt honored to get an invitation to her parties. She also hosted dinner parties for Donald, his associates, and clients. Her dinners were legendary. Of course, she had help with all of these activities. She had a maid that did all the cooking and cleaning, though Susan accepted the accolades.

Susan was also president of the Garden Society. Though her gardener deserved the praise for his hard work that grew the brilliant flowers that bloomed beside her house. She would wear her gloves and flit around the garden once a week with her scissors, cutting blooms for her renowned flower arrangements.

Donald worked hard at his advertising job to provide the best for Susan and she was very grateful for it. It did seem that he had to work harder and harder each month and stayed later and later. But he never complained or explained and she never asked questions as to why. She just accepted her life for what it was and went on about it.

One day, late in November, Susan was called to the phone by her maid. Who could possibly be calling her at this late hour? It was so impolite and she was tempted to tell them so. She picked up the receiver and spat out a sharp 'yes', hoping to embarrass the caller.

"Susan? Susan, is that you?" said the anxious voice on the other end of the line.

"Of course, it is! Who is this may I ask?" she said tersely.

"Susan, this is Bob Tillman. There's been an incident here at work. I walked in to Donald's office and found him lying on the floor. I called an ambulance and they're on their way but it looks bad. I think you need to go to the hospital right away."

She stood there holding the receiver. A million thoughts ran through her head. *What will I do? Who will pay the bills? The gardener? The maid? I have that Relief Society meeting this week, do I cancel it? He has to get better, doesn't he? Surely, it's not as bad as Bob thinks. He probably just fell asleep and fell out of his chair.* "I'll be right there, Bob. Thank you for calling," and she hung up the phone.

"Louisa, Mr. Donald will not be home for dinner and will you please keep mine warm for me?

I am stepping out and will be back in a couple of hours," she called to her maid as she started up the stairs to change clothes.

Susan took her own sweet time getting ready. She couldn't present herself at the hospital looking like a shrew and wearing something she just threw on. She put on her blue striped shirtwaist dress with the patent leather belt. Heels or ballerina flats? Heels would look more imposing if she should need it. She put on her makeup and teased her hair. There, that would just have to do.

An hour later, Susan arrived at the hospital and looked for Donald. She stopped at the front desk and asked the frazzled nurse where she could find him. Once she said his name, the expression on the nurse's face changed. She stood up, not quite making eye contact with Susan.

"Please have a seat, ma'am, and I will get the doctor for you," the nurse instructed her kindly.

"I don't want to have a seat. I want to see my husband. Take me to him right now," said Susan haughtily as the nurse kept walking.

A few minutes later, the doctor came down the hall. His eyes were downcast and Susan could not read his expression. "I want to see my husband," she stated. "Take me to him right now," she demanded.

"Please sit down," the doctor instructed Susan as he waited patiently to take his own seat. "I'm afraid I have some bad news. Your husband suffered a severe heart attack. We were unable to resuscitate him in the emergency room. I am sorry to tell you, he passed away about half an hour ago."

Susan just stared at the doctor in shock. *Donald gone? How could that be? He was just sitting at the breakfast table this morning. What am I going to do?* "Doctor, are you sure?"

"Yes, ma'am. I'm sorry to say I am. Is there anyone we can call for you?"

"No, thank you. You have done quite enough." And with that, Susan stood up and walked out of the hospital.

Susan planned a beautiful, lavish funeral for Donald as befitted their status in the community.

After everyone had paid their respects and left the house, Susan sat down weary from all the work she had done.

"Can I get you anything, Miss Susan?" Louisa asked as she worked to clean up the mess left behind.

"No, thank you, Louisa. Just finish cleaning up and that will be all for today."

Within two weeks, Susan was getting bills in the mail. Bills she didn't have a clue how to deal with. Then the funeral bills began to come in, exorbitant bills. Without Donald's income, how was she to pay these? Susan turned to their friend and lawyer, Darrin, to help her sort everything out.

"Darrin, when can I collect Donald's insurance? I have bills to pay," Susan asked.

"Um, Susan, didn't Donald tell you? He cashed in his insurance policy months ago. He said he needed the money. I am so sorry. There is no money. Didn't he have a savings account set aside for you?" Darrin asked as he looked down at his hands.

"No, there isn't any money anywhere I can find. The bank accounts only have enough to pay the house bills for one month. It doesn't leave any for my maid or the gardener. There's not even enough to get my hair done. What am I supposed to do?" she asked in desperation.

Darrin continued to look down at his hands. "Um, I don't know, Susan. I cautioned Donald about his spending but he was determined to keep up appearances even when his finances would not support it."

"What happened to all our money, Darrin? Do you know? Please tell me."

"I don't want to speak ill of the dead, but Donald did confess that he had started gambling some nights. I believe he got in too deep and owed too many people money."

"Gambling? Donald wouldn't. He wouldn't have left me like this. How could he? Oh, I'll never forgive him, never!"

"I'm sorry, Susan, but there's more. I'm afraid he took out a second mortgage on the house and there is no money left to pay it. It looks like you will need to move by the end of the month. I'm afraid you will have to get a job, too. There is simply no other choice."

Susan burst into tears. "How could he do this to me? I hate him. Do you hear that Donald? I hate you! I will hate you till the day I die!"

Darrin went over and cautiously patted Susan on the shoulder. "I'm sorry to be the bearer of such bad news. I'll let myself out now and if you need me, you know where to find me."

Susan couldn't move. She was devastated. It was bad enough to lose Louisa and the house. But to have to get a job. No one in her clubs had a job. No one she knew had a job. Oh, the humiliation! She didn't even know where to start. *Oh, that Donald!*

The month ended all too soon. The gardener had already been snapped up by one of her friends and Louisa was still deciding between two others for her next employment.

Louisa's last day was a sad one for them both. Susan hugged her, wished her the best, and thanked her for her dedication and hard work. She even cried, whether it was for the loss of her maid or for herself, she didn't know. "Oh, Louisa, what will I do? I have to move and I can't find a house anywhere. Then I have to get a job. I don't know how to do anything except give parties and where will that get me?"

Louisa gave her employer a pat on the hand and timidly said that she might know of a small house that Susan could afford. She also knew of a job opening, but she wasn't sure how Susan would feel about it.

"Where is this house, Louisa? How big is it? Does it have a garden? Who do I need to talk to about it?" Susan asked desperately.

Louisa said she would set up a meeting with the owner, Mr. O'Shaunessy, tomorrow if Susan wanted her to. She also mentioned the job opening she had heard about.

"What is the job, Louisa? Is it something you think I could do? Is it easy? Does it pay good? What can you tell me about it?" Susan asked excitedly.

"Well, I am not sure if it is something you would want to do, but it should be fairly easy. I'm also not sure about the pay. That is something you would have to work out with Mr. Lawson if you got the job."

"What is it, Louisa, tell me. I'll do just about anything right now."

"It's for a housekeeper for Mr. Max Lawson. He is an architect that is new in town. He works late hours. You would need to have dinner ready and waiting for him in the oven every night. What do you think, Miss Susan?"

"Now, Louisa, no more Miss Susan. It's just Susan, please. If you would set up a meeting with me and Mr. O'Shaunessy and another with Mr. Lawson, I would greatly appreciate it." *Oh, how the mighty have fallen. A housekeeper of all things!*

After Louisa left, Susan dragged herself up the steps to the bedroom. She had already packed up her clothes, though what she would need with them as a housekeeper she had no idea. She knew nothing about housekeeping except what she had observed Louisa doing. Well, she was just going to have to fake it.

Susan got up the next morning determined to take care of business. She had a ten o'clock appointment to see the little house and a lunch meeting with Mr. Lawson to discuss the housekeeper job. She put on a very simple skirt and sweater set, she wanted to look the part of a housekeeper.

She climbed into the baby blue Ford Thunderbird convertible, a present from Donald for their last anniversary and left for her first appointment. It was unseasonably warm, so she let the top down. She had to turn around several times before she located the tiny, overgrown path that was Dragonfly Lane. The car bumped along the long road as low hanging branches snagged at her carefully arranged hair do. As she pulled up to the little cottage, with its welcoming green front door, something inside her began to lift. That hard stone of resentment slightly loosened its grip.

There was a small, round man standing at the door. He had silver hair and was dressed in a suit, very old fashioned, and complete with a bow tie. He also wore a bowler hat and was carrying a cane. She assumed this was Mr. O'Shaunessy as she couldn't imagine who else would be out in this God forsaken place.

As she walked up the path, the little man took off his hat and bowed in greeting.

"Mrs. Taylor or may I call you Susan?" he inquired in a voice with some accent Susan could not place.

"Yes, please. And you must be Mr. O'Shaunessy? It's a pleasure to meet you."

"Indeed, a pleasure. Would you like to take a tour of the cottage? I think it will be just what you are looking for."

They walked into the first room and Susan was thankful for the fire burning in the little stove as the wind had unexpectedly sprung up and it had turned colder under all those trees. Mr. O'Shaunessy led her through the rooms and proudly pointed out all the necessary details. He was especially proud of the kitchen and bathroom, that even though still quaint, had all the necessities.

"The cottage does come furnished, complete with pots and pans, but if you would like to bring your own things, I can get this stuff moved into storage," he offered.

Susan tried to hide as she cringed at the thought of her beautiful furnishings in the tiny little rooms. "No, that won't be necessary. I am not bringing any of my furniture with me. This will be just fine."

Mr. O'Shaunessy smiled widely. "Fine, fine. A wise decision as you will have much less to move. Do you need any help moving anything? I know some fine lads that I could get to help you."

"No, that's very kind, but I only have my clothes and books. I can fit them in my car."

"Well, what do you think? Will this suffice?"

"Yes, it will have to," she blurted out before thinking.

Mr. O'Shaunessy pretended not to notice. He held out a key, one of those long, thin metal ones that looked from the early 1900's, and placed it in her hand. "Well, we're all done then. I collect the rent on the first of every month. We can waive the first month if you need that time to get settled in. There is always some kind of unexpected expense that comes up it seems."

Unexpectedly, tears welled up in Susan's eyes. This show of kindness took her off guard. Since news of her change of circumstances, her friends had distanced themselves from her, as if her misfortune could rub off on them. Strangely, this betrayal stung worse than the death of her husband.

"Thank you for your kindness. I will take you up on your generous offer. I am applying for a job this afternoon, and my hope is to start next week."

"Well, I wish you the best of luck on that and I will let you take your time looking over the place before you leave," Mr. O'Shaunessy said with a wink.

Susan straightened her hair in the bathroom mirror, even pulling a few twigs out of her bouffant hairdo. Locking the green door, she walked over and put the top up on the convertible before she left for her appointment. On the trip back out, the lane had not seemed so long and winding as the first time. But she did notice that there was no sign of the little house from the road. It was almost as if it disappeared when no one was there. Strange.

She drove quickly to a little diner. She arrived a few minutes early and sprung for a cup of coffee to calm her nerves. Mr. Lawson arrived promptly at noon, sat down, and ordered a coffee for himself and a sandwich to go. Susan learned the diner was only a block from Mr. Lawson's office. He had carved out precious time from his schedule to interview Susan. This was definitely in her favor. Precious little time meant he would be more desperate to hurry and hire someone.

"I apologize for the rush of this interview, but I am in the middle of a very important project and I can't afford to be gone too long. Now, let's get started. I must say Mrs. Martin spoke very highly of you. She gave you a glowing review."

Mrs. Martin, who was he talking about? Could that be Louisa? Funny, I never knew her last name. Unsure of what to say, Susan just smiled and sipped her coffee.

"Now, what I am looking for is someone who can keep my household up and running while I am busy at the office. I will need the house kept clean and everything that entails. I am not sure what all that would be, but I trust you do."

Susan continued to give him a little smile but this time she nodded her head as if she understood exactly what he meant.

"I will also need you to grocery shop and keep the kitchen well stocked. I am usually home late, so I would require dinner to be left in the oven for me. I would need laundry done weekly and my suits taken to the cleaners. On nights when I entertain clients, I would need you to stay late and assist. Does this sound like something you would be interested in?"

Susan realized it was her time to speak. "Yes, yes it does. I feel that I am perfect for the job. I have run a large household before and am confident that I can run yours for you. *No need to tell him that while I ran the household, I did not, in fact, do any of the work.* "I would appreciate the opportunity Mr. Lawson and will do my best."

Max looked her up and down, taking in the fancy hairdo and matching skirt and sweater. He began to have doubts, but time was money right now and he couldn't afford to drag out this hunt for a housekeeper any longer than necessary. "Okay, Mrs. Taylor. If you are agreeable, let's give this a one-month trial. You can start this Saturday morning about nine. That way I will be able to show you around the house and answer any questions you may have. I will have to go in to work after that. What do you say?" He was standing up and leaving money on the table for the coffees and sandwich.

"That would be fine, Mr. Lawson. I'll see you Saturday at nine o'clock and thank you for this opportunity."

"I'll see you then. It was nice to meet you, Mrs. Taylor. I need to get back to the office. Take care." And he ran out the door.

Susan got a refill of coffee and sat thinking about how her life had completely changed in the last couple of months. She had lost her house, her maid, and her husband and mourned them in that order. But thanks to Louisa, she now had a new place to live and a job. Who would have thought that she would now be dependent on her maid's advice?

She realized she had plenty of time to move her things into the cottage and settle in. She wasn't taking very much, it would probably fit in the trunk of the Thunderbird. The Thunderbird. That too was a luxury she could no longer afford. How would it look pulling up at her housekeeper's job in such a fancy car? No, it was time to sell it. She took a deep, quivering breath. No looking back. It must go.

Three hours later, the Thunderbird was gone and Susan was now the proud owner of a much used, dark green, four door Chevy Bel-Air. She took what remained of the sale and bought proper housemaid clothes. She went to the bargain basement of Parks Belk, somewhere she had never stepped foot in before, and shopped for uniforms, dresses, skirts, and sensible shoes.

Susan actually cried when she left with her purchases. She believed this hurt most of all.

The next morning, Susan dressed in her oldest clothes and loaded up the Chevy with her books and the clothes from her old life. Why she kept them, she had no idea except she just couldn't bear to part with such beauty. Who knew? Maybe one day she would again have an opportunity to wear them. A girl could dream, couldn't she? At least that didn't cost anything.

Once again, she missed the turn off to Dragonfly Lane, but only once this time. The old Chevy nearly bounced her teeth out driving over the potholes. She resolved to talk to Mr. O'Shaunessy about that the next time she saw him. The sun shone through the trees today in a rare late fall appearance and Susan was grateful. In fact, the little cottage fairly glowed from the rays of sunlight bouncing off its red brick walls. Susan stopped the car a little way back and just sat there looking at it. It really wasn't a bad little house and she was incredibly lucky to have it.

Moving along, she parked and drug her belongings out of the trunk. It only took a couple of trips and she was done.

She went back and pulled several grocery bags out of the back seat. She had the box of recipes Louisa had given her before she left and now was as good a time as any to try her hand at cooking. Louisa, bless her heart, had arranged the recipes in order of difficulty. First in line was sweet tea and cornbread. Susan read the recipes and decided they sounded fairly easy. She dug out a pan and a skillet, going by the descriptions that she had kindly provided, and after fumbling around, she managed to turn on the stove and oven.

The tea was easy. Boil the water, put in the tea bags, stir in a cup of sugar and wait. The cornbread was a little trickier but she finally managed to get it in the oven. A little later, Susan sat down to her first meal and was pretty pleased with herself. The cornbread was a little bit burned on the bottom, but she resolved to do better next time. After all, she had four more days to learn to cook well. How hard could it be?

Susan spent those next four days cooking. She had to make two more trips to the grocery store, as she ruined as many dishes as she got right. But by Friday night, she felt confident that she could cook a simple meal for Mr. Lawson. At least, if he wasn't terribly picky.

Saturday started with a downpour which completely matched her mood. She absolutely hated her new clothes and the sturdy shoes were atrocious. She was drenched by the time she got to her car and her hair, which was now cut to a sensible pixie cut, made her look like a drowned rat. Oh well, hopefully the day wouldn't get any worse.

Mr. Lawson opened the front door with a surprised look on his face. Okay, admittedly she did look different than when he first saw her, but not that different.

He looked down at the growing puddle of water on his living room carpet and stated "I'll give you a key to the side door for the future."

Susan was mortified. It had never crossed her mind that help did not use the front door, but no, Louisa had never used hers. Another unpleasant reminder of how low her life had become.

"I'm so sorry for the mess. If you'll show me where the mop and towels are, I'll clean all this up."

After she mopped up the water, he took Susan on a tour of the house. It was quite large for only one person, and seemed like quite a lot to keep clean. The kitchen had the same gadgets as Susan's old kitchen, so she should be able to at least guess at their use.

"Mr. Lawson, when will you be wanting supper ready this evening?"

"I will probably be home late, so if you'll just leave a plate in the oven that will be fine."

Susan let out a sigh of relief when he left. Now she could explore the house on her own and try to see what all she would need to do. She couldn't keep herself from commenting on the horrible decorating job. Maybe she could rearrange the furniture into a more pleasing arrangement.

She let out a shriek when the doorbell rang. Who on earth would be visiting at this hour? She slowly opened the door and was surprised to see Louisa standing on the doorstep.

"Louisa, what are you doing here?"

"I thought you could use some help on your first day, Miss Susan. I can show you some of my cleaning tricks and help you get that meal started."

Susan did not know what to say. She stood there with her mouth open. Then she reached out and grabbed Louisa's hand and pulled her in. She gave her a quick and spontaneous hug. Stepping back, her cheeks burned with embarrassment.

"I'm sorry. I'm just so glad to see you. I am totally confused as where to start."

"Well, you just get some paper and write down what I say. Then when it's time for you to do it on your own, you'll know exactly what to do."

Susan took meticulous notes as Louisa walked her through all the tasks involved in keeping a house. At noon, they took a break and shared a cup of coffee at the kitchen table. Susan believed it was the first time she had done this in all the time Louisa had worked for her. She really enjoyed getting to know more about the woman and wished she had taken the time to know her before this.

"Why are you so nice to me, Louisa? I realize now I was not the easiest person to work for. Why would you spend one of your days off to come help me?"

Louisa just smiled, "Well, Miss Susan..."

Susan interrupted, "After all you've done for me, please just call me Susan."

"Susan," Louisa said awkwardly. "You were a little 'difficult' to work for sometimes, but you were never unkind. You are in a tough situation and I just want to help you get your feet back under you. You've been dealt a lot of tough blows and not everyone would try to pick themselves up like you are. You are a brave woman."

Susan blushed. She knew all the hateful thoughts she had been having lately and felt unworthy of the compliment.

"Now, it's time to get that supper started. Get that paper ready." Susan took so many notes that by the time they were done, she had a whole notebook full of instructions, shortcuts, and new recipes. "I can't thank you enough, Louisa. You are a life saver!"

"Well, you just call on me whenever you get stuck and I'll help you out. If I'm not available, the other girls said they would be glad to help you. I've written down their phone numbers for you."

It was all she could do to hold back tears. No one had ever been so kind to her before, even her fancy club friends. Why would these women be willing to help her? They didn't even know her. What kind of people were they to help out a perfect stranger who could do nothing for them? Susan couldn't understand, but she would like to learn more about these ladies.

As if reading her mind, Louisa said, "We all meet Sunday afternoons at the diner in town. We're all off work and we like to get together to talk and pray about the upcoming week. You are more than welcome to join us. The girls would love to meet you and share their hints with you."

Not sure if she was ready for that yet, she smiled and nodded her head. "Maybe I will do that after I get settled in. I would really like to thank them for their kindness."

Louisa made sure Susan had everything she needed to finish up dinner before she left. Susan gave her another hug, less awkward this time, and felt she had found a friend for the first time in a long time. She still didn't understand exactly the reason Louisa helped her, but she wanted to learn more.

That evening, she went home and fell into bed. She was utterly exhausted. She was so grateful to have the day off. After sleeping till noon, she practiced her breakfast making skills using some of the hints Louisa had given her. Then she straightened up the little house and tried to make it feel a little bit more like her home, whether she liked it or not. While she worked, she reflected on all that had happened this past week and how much her life had changed. It was different for sure, but not as heartbreaking as she had once assumed. She also thought a lot about Louisa and her kindness. She still couldn't figure it all out.

Monday morning rolled around all too fast and Susan had to force herself out of bed. Her body ached all over and all she wanted was to roll over and go back to sleep. But she had a job to do, ugh, and do it she must. She put back on the dreaded maid outfit and shoes and ran out the door, making it to the house right on time. Thankfully, Mr. Lawson had already left for work and she had the house all to herself. She pulled out her notes and got busy. There really wasn't that much to do around the house except pick up clothes, make the bed, and straighten the bathroom. Mr. Lawson was not the neatest, but then that was her job now, wasn't it?

Soon, it was time to start dinner and she stared at her recipe cards, in complete confusion. It was as if she had forgotten everything she had practiced. She couldn't even remember how to make iced tea. In desperation, she called Louisa. The phone just rang and rang. Now what? She looked at the numbers of the other maids. Would they really be willing to help her out? Did she trust that they would do something for her when she couldn't return the favor? Shakily, she dialed the first number.

It was answered on the first ring. "Cummings residence, how may I help you?"

Susan froze, unsure what to say. "Um, may I speak to Frances? This is Susan. Louisa said to call her if I needed any help."

"This is Frances and of course, I'd be glad to help you Susan. What are you having trouble with today?"

"I have to start dinner and I can't think of a thing to cook. My mind is blank. I've forgotten everything Louisa taught me."

"Oh, I'm sure you haven't forgotten it all. It's just a lot to take in all at once. Let's start with something easy."

Frances walked Susan through all the steps to start a hearty pot of soup and a pitcher of iced tea. "Now, you call Martha and she can walk you through how to make a cobbler. Martha makes the best cobbler in three counties."

"I can't thank you enough for your help, Frances. I feel much calmer now. I can't imagine what I would do without you and Louisa."

"Now, honey, don't you think a thing of it. We are always ready to lend a helping hand. You don't ever hesitate to call any time."

Susan hung up and immediately called Martha. She too answered on the first ring and was more than happy to help out with the dessert.

Leaving everything in the oven for Mr. Lawson, Susan walked slowly to her car. She wondered at her day and the kindness of the women. What made these women so special? What made them so ready to help out?

The weeks flew by and Susan grew more confidant. With the help of the various ladies, she had managed to not only clean the house, but do the laundry, and fix a variety of dishes. Mr. Lawson left a note praising her cooking and that he felt their arrangement was working out nicely.

At the end of the second month, Mr. Lawson was still there when she arrived and Susan began to feel apprehensive.

"Susan, I feel like things have worked out very well here, don't you?"

"Yes, sir. I do."

"They are going so well, I have decided to have a dinner party with some of the men from my firm and their wives so I can get to know them better. How does Friday night sound? Nothing too fancy, but just fancy enough to impress. I will pay you overtime, of course."

Susan didn't know what to say. She just smiled and nodded. As soon as he left, she called Louisa in a panic. "He wants to have a dinner party Friday night. He wants something fancy enough to impress. He wants me to serve. What am I going to do?"

"Now calm down. The girls and I will all pitch in and help. We will all make a different dish and you just have to keep them warm or cold until time to serve. I can come over every day on my lunch break and teach you how to serve. It's really very easy, so stay calm and I'll see you at noon."

Louisa was true to her word and came over every day and instructed Susan how to serve. She learned to serve from the left but to pick up the used dishes from the nearest side. She learned how to properly set the table and how to serve the coffee after dinner. The other ladies sent word of what dishes they would make and the dinner slowly came together. Susan began to calm down. The women had once again come to her rescue and she still had nothing to repay them with, though they didn't seem to expect it.

Friday came and Susan spent the morning making sure the house was spotless. After Mr. Lawson's kindness, she wanted to make sure he would impress his co-workers. All day, the ladies made the trip to drop off the dishes they had made. As day turned to dusk, Susan changed into the outfit Louisa had loaned her and set about arranging the dishes in the order to be served.

Mr. Lawson came home and complimented her on the wonderful smells coming from the kitchen. He ran upstairs to change into the suit she had freshly pressed for him and left out on the bed. She double checked the dining room and was proud of how it turned out. Everything seemed to be falling into place.

The guests began arriving at six and Mr. Lawson answered the door to greet them. Susan was busy in the kitchen and anxiously awaited the word from him to begin serving dinner. Promptly at seven, Mr. Lawson announced for everyone to come into the dining room. It was show time for Susan.

Her hands shook a little as she began to serve the soup. Thank goodness it was a cold soup and didn't shake too much in the bowl. Everything was going well until Susan locked eyes with the second wife she served. It was her former co-chairman of the Relief Society. She had actually taken over when Susan had resigned. Suddenly, she didn't know what to do or where to look. Mr. Lawson discreetly cleared his throat and that broke the spell. She calmly placed the bowl down in front of her friend and moved on around the table. She then noticed another wife from the Relief Society. Why, oh why, hadn't she thought of this possibility? She was absolutely mortified and didn't think she could continue. How could she serve these women who used to be her friends? Even though they had lost contact when her circumstances changed, she still considered them friends.

Susan cleared plates and served the remaining courses, never making eye contact again with anyone except Mr. Lawson. His smile assured her things were going well for him even though she wished the earth would open and swallow her up. She had never been so embarrassed in her life and she knew her cheeks burned bright red. She thought this was the absolute worst until after dinner when she had to serve coffee and dessert. The ladies she had considered her friends began to talk to Mr. Lawson as if she weren't there or at least that she couldn't hear. They asked

when he had hired her, where he had found her, and how she was working out. Had she been so thoughtless in front of Louisa? Had she talked about her as if she wasn't there? Susan was horrified and she cheeks burned even brighter. Not so much at these women's rude remarks, but at her own heartlessness to someone who had only shown kindness to her.

The evening seemed to last forever, but finally it was time for Susan to retrieve all the coats as Mr. Lawson bade them all farewell. As she cleaned up the kitchen, he came in brimming with compliments. He told her the dinner was excellent and she had done an excellent job serving his guests and to take the next day off. He would fend for himself the next two days.

Susan finished up and slowly made her way to her car. She had never been so exhausted. When she got home, she fell into bed too tired to even undress but her mind would not give her rest. She thought about her former friends and how they acted. It was embarrassing to serve them but to talk about her after dinner, as if she were some kind of inanimate object unable to hear or speak. How could they be so cruel? They once fawned all over her and called her their best and closest friend? Well, they were just, they were just two-faced, that's what they were! And mean. How had she not noticed that before? Had she been like them? Had she been cruel and thoughtless to others? Her mind went around and round reliving the past few years with shame and regret. She finally fell asleep as the sun rose over the little cottage.

Saturday afternoon was spent resting and tidying up the cottage. She had also been tending a small garden discovered out back and was pleased to note how neat it looked without the dead plants. She sent a silent thank you to the former tenants for having left her something to connect her to her old life. If she had realized how healing it was to take care of the plants herself, she would have done so long ago. She now regretted all the time she spent arranging the flowers instead of appreciating them for their beauty, resilience, and tenacity. Something she hoped to find in her new life.

Sunday dawned and she woke rested and refreshed. The house was clean and the garden tended and she was at a loss as to what to do. The whole day stretched before her and she felt something she hadn't in a long time, contentment. Then she remembered the women gathered at the diner on Sunday afternoons and she suddenly felt the need to go. Would they be as friendly and welcoming as they had been all month or would they suddenly treat her like a former employer? Did she really want to risk finding out? Well, she had survived Friday night when she didn't think she could, so she would face however these women acted. She decided to go.

Susan hesitantly walked into the diner. As she looked around for the group, she heard someone call out her name. She turned around and spotted the group of women at a large table, beckoning for her to come over.

"Susan, we're so glad you could join us!" Martha said. "We're all so anxious to hear how your first dinner party went. Sit down and tell us all about it."

"Now at least give her enough time to get a cup of coffee before we hound her for details," Louisa said.

Susan, grateful for a moment to gather her thoughts and decide if she wanted to tell all, sat down and ordered. Then taking a deep breath, she sighed. The women looked at her concerned.

When the waitress dropped off the coffee, Susan took a deep breath and began. "All your dishes were a big hit. Everyone went mad over the variety, the taste, and the presentation. I can't thank you enough for all you've done to help me this past month. You have all been so kind and I can truly say that I don't deserve any of it. Let me just apologize now if I have ever been unkind or thoughtless toward any of you. I am truly sorry if I have ever made you feel anything less than the wonderful, giving women that you are."

The women sat in silence, glancing at each other in concern. Something bad had happened and now they just needed to wait and see if Susan would feel comfortable enough to share with them.

Susan took a deep breath. Did she trust these women enough to share with them? Would they understand the betrayal? Would they feel like she was belittling them or their positions?

"Susan, we are all here for you if you feel like sharing. We are not here to judge in any way, so if you feel comfortable enough..."

Looking at all the concerned faces around the table, Susan began the story that weighed heavy on her mind. "The dinner was going just fine until I saw two ladies from my former Relief Society group."

There was a collective groan.

"Susan, how horrible for you. Please tell us they behaved with grace and respect," Frances said.

Louisa reached out and patted Susan on the shoulder.

Susan's eyes filled with tears. She was embarrassed and ashamed of her previous beliefs and former friends. Hesitantly, she began to tell how the two ladies talked about her and around her after the dinner. She told how they asked embarrassing questions about her to Mr. Lawson while she was serving them each coffee.

Somehow, as she told the story, while humiliating, brought a sense of healing. The women alternatively gasped, sighed, and even cried. It was as if the sharing brought them closer together. They all began to share their own humiliating stories and Susan felt a sense of relief.

Here she is with women whom she used to consider beneath her notice and yet she felt closer to them than her former 'friends'. What was happening to her and all her former beliefs? It felt like her life had turned upside down. But yet, it felt like her life may be turning out like it should have been all along.

With an afternoon spent sharing, the ladies separated but all managed to give Susan a warm hug and some parting words of encouragement. She left with new found friendships and renewed hope.

When she arrived home, strange how she called it home now, she took a walk down the lane and thought about her life. She was still shocked at the actions of her former friends and couldn't believe their cruelty for the sake of being cruel. But she was also thankful for her new friends and the love they had poured out on her. She learned today that they truly did not expect anything from her in return. They had given their friendship and help freely. Suddenly, she remembered the Sunday school classes from when she was a kid and they began to make sense. God's love was reflected in those ladies today and their kindness.

Donald, how sorry she felt now for all the bad things she had said and thought about him. While many things had happened were his responsibility to bear, many were hers and she could see that now. She should have paid more attention. She should have seen the strain he was under trying to keep up appearances. She should have talked to him more. She asked out loud for his forgiveness and felt a heaviness lift from her heart from all the resentment she had carried for so long.

Strange, what she thought had ruined her life had actually made her life richer.

Sandy and Richard

The 1960s

Sandy met Richard, or Richie as everyone called him, at the Dairy Dip on a Friday night after the big game. Sandy was a cheerleader and had always been attracted to football types until she saw the tall, dark headed young man behind the window at the Dip. He shot her a glance as she stepped up to the window and ordered and she had never seen eyes so blue. She stammered as she ordered even more food, way too much for one person, hoping he would look up again. He did, and his eyes crinkled in amusement.

Feeling awkward, she took a step back and went to the other window to pay. She couldn't help but notice his eyes still followed her. Who was this guy? Where did he come from? She had never noticed him before. He looked a few years older than her, so what was he doing working the grill at the local Dairy Dip?

Sandy got her order and went to the table where her friends waited.

"What took you so long? And what on earth are you doing with all this food?" Karen asked.

"Have y'all seen the dreamboat working the grill? He reminds me of Elvis and his eyes, his eyes are this deep, deep shade of blue," Sandy gushed. "Does anyone know his name?"

"Come on Sandy. You can have any boy on the football team. Why are you mooning over some fry guy?"

"I don't know, there's just something about him. I can't put my finger on it, but something about him interests me."

The other girls went up to the window under the pretext of getting ketchup, more napkins, or a straw just to get a glimpse of the guy in question.

They all agreed that he was indeed good looking, but was he a good catch compared to the quarterback of the football team? They didn't think so.

At 9:45, everyone cleared off the trash and got ready to go. "You coming Sandy?"

"No, I think I'll hang around a little while longer. I'll call y'all tomorrow, okay?" And with that, Sandy settled herself at the table and prepared herself to wait until the handsome guy got off work. She pulled out a book and pretended to read, only glimpsing up occasionally to check on him.

At eleven, the inside lights of the Dip turned off and the employees began to trickle out. Even though Sandy worried about getting in trouble with her parents for being late, she wouldn't leave until she had at least learned the mysterious stranger's name.

"You know we're closing now," came a low voice behind Sandy.

She jumped but quickly gained her composure. "Oh, I must have gotten lost in my book and forgot all about the time," she attempted in an innocent voice. "What a clunk head I am."

He smiled a quick smile, showing off a mouthful of bright white teeth. She thought he could be on TV if he wanted to. He was that good looking.

"What are you reading," he asked as he sat down opposite her.

"To Kill a Mockingbird, it's for a senior school project," she said hastily, unless he thought her a nerd who read books just for fun.

"Great book," he said. "I had to read it my senior year too. My name's Richard, but my friends call me Richie," he said extending his hand.

"Hi, Richie, my name is Sandy," she clasped his hand and felt a jolt of electricity travel between them.

She turned her head to hide the look of shock on her face. No one had ever made her feel that way before. Those boys from school looked like children compared to him. "I've never seen you here before. When did you start work at the Dip?"

"I just started this week. My aunt lives here in town and she said I could live here until I know what I want to do with my life. I graduated last year and have tried out several jobs but can't decide exactly what I like. I just know college is not for me."

Sandy nodded her head in agreement. "I know I don't want to go to college either. I guess I'll get married and become a housewife. That's what everyone seems to be doing," then thinking that may have sounded leading, she quickly changed the subject. "I guess I need to go on home."

"I'd be happy to drive you. My car is right over there." And he pointed to a beat-up old Ford, more rust than paint. "I can leave as soon as I pick up these tables."

"Okay, I'll help you." They continued to talk as they worked. They hit on all the little subjects two people talk about when getting to know each other. Soon they were in his car and Sandy gave him directions to her house.

He walked her to the door and being a gentleman, did not kiss her. Though Sandy would like to see if that jolt of electricity worked for a kiss too.

"Can I see you tomorrow night? I get off at 5. We could go to the movies. 'The Magnificent Seven' is playing."

Sandy couldn't say yes fast enough. Now she had to make sure her parents would approve.

"Um, you'll have to come meet my parents first. Is that okay?" she asked hesitantly. She suddenly felt like a baby.

"Of course. I wouldn't dream of taking you out without meeting them first. I'll be here at six o'clock. Is that okay? That way we can get a sandwich before the movie."

"Yes, that will be perfect," Sandy said, relieved. Now to pray that her parents' will like him and let her go.

Sandy then closed the door and leaned against it in a partial swoon. She had a date with the handsomest man she had ever seen. He seemed more mature than the other boys she had gone out with. She ran up the stairs to call Karen and give her all the details.

Richie arrived promptly at six o'clock and Sandy's dad beat her to answer the door.

"Come in young man," he said as he extended his hand. "Are we to understand that you want to take out our little Sandy?"

Richie shook his hand firmly. "Yes sir."

"Well, have a seat Richard and tell us a little about yourself."

Sandy cringed. Here comes the third degree. But Richie seemed to take it all in stride.

"My name is Richard Morrison and I am originally from Memphis. My mother still lives there, my dad was killed in action during the war."

"I'm sorry to hear that, son. We lost a lot of good men in that war," he paused. "What are your plans for the future? Do you intend to make a career of flipping burgers?"

Richard smiled and told her parents of his time spent trying out different jobs to find one that suited him. He assured them that the hamburger joint was temporary until a job at the factory opened up.

What seemed like an eternity passed when her father stood up and said "You kids better get a move on, or you'll miss the opening credits."

Sandy grabbed Richie's hand and pulled him out the door. "I'm sorry about all the questions. They are so old fashioned, practically from the stone age."

"Oh, I think it's sweet how protective they are. They only want the best for you. I didn't mind really."

They were running late, so decided to have popcorn for supper. They both shared a laugh at the ridiculous ads with the dancing food and commented on the upcoming movies they would both like to see next. As if it were understood there would be a 'next' date.

At the end of the night, Richie asked if he could kiss her and Sandy quickly nodded her head. That same jolt of electricity that had happened when their hands met was even more intense when their lips met. They both sat back in surprise.

"Wow," was all they could both seem to say.

"Did you feel it to?" he asked, his voice shaking just a little.

"Yes."

They both broke into a big smile.

And that's how their love story began.

Sandy's senior year went by in a flash. Richie was her date to homecoming and prom. He looked so handsome in his dark blue suit which matched the sash to her dress and the ribbon on her white rose corsage.

He brought her a dozen roses when she graduated and all the other girls admitted they were jealous.

Richie had gotten that job at the factory and while he made more money, it still did not satisfy that longing he felt for something more. Sandy could tell he was getting more restless but she didn't know how to help him. She prayed that he would not get restless and leave her. That was her greatest fear.

A few months after graduation, Richie picked Sandy up in his now repainted jalopy for a date at the Dairy Dip. After ordering their usual, they found a table and took a seat. When the order was ready, Richie carried the tray to the table and sat it over away from Sandy. She turned to look at him in confusion and noticed that he had gone down on one knee.

"Sandy, I know this seems like an unusual place to do this, but since it's where I first fell in love with you, I don't know, it just felt right somehow." He reached into his pocket and pulled out a small box tied with a dark blue ribbon. His hand shook as he held it out to her. "Will you do me the great honor of becoming my wife?" he stammered.

Sandy jumped up and flung her arms around his neck as the other people at the Dip began clapping.

"Well, is that a yes?"

"Yes, yes, yes!" she shouted.

Over the next few months, wedding preparations, the gown, the colors, and where they would live afterwards were constant topics of conversation. One day, Richie came to pick up Sandy and he had a big grin on his face.

"What are you up to?" she asked. "You look like the cat that swallowed the canary."

"Oh, nothing much. I just want to take you for a ride is all. Now hop in the car and let's get going. We have to meet somebody in about fifteen minutes and we don't want to be late."

Richie drove across town and turned down a small, overgrown gravel lane. Trees seemed to encroach on what little bit of road there was and Richie's big, old Ford slapped at the tree branches. When they pulled into the little clearing, there sat a small red brick cottage with a green door. Standing in front was a little man with a hat and cane.

Helping Sandy out of the car, Richie said, "Mr. O'Shaunessy, it's good to see you again, sir. This is my soon to be wife, Sandy Harrison. It was very nice of you to meet us here this afternoon. I wanted Sandy to see the cottage before we shook on the deal."

"I understand, I understand," Mr. O'Shaunessy said. "The door is open. Take your time and show Miss Harrison around the house. I'll wait here. Please let me know if you have any questions."

With that, Richie took Sandy's hand and like a young boy with a toy, he begins to show Sandy around the cottage. He started with the main room and ended with the garden out back. He pointed out the house's good points and his visions of what they could make of it. His excitement was contagious and soon Sandy was laughing and picturing them there too.

Mr. O'Shaunessy smiled as the couple came out the front door. "I take it everything met with your approval?"

"Oh, yes sir!" Sandy exclaimed. "It is absolutely perfect."

Richie reached over and shook the man's hand. "You've got a deal, sir. We think this is the perfect house to start our life together."

Mr. O'Shaunessy pulled an old-fashioned key off his key ring and handed it over to Richie. They agreed on the rent, when it was to be paid, and when they could move in.

"Congratulations you two. I wish you the best of luck on your upcoming marriage and your future life together." With that, he started walking down the lane and was soon out of sight.

Richie picked up Sandy and spun her around. "Now let's get this wedding going. I can't wait to make you Mrs. Richard Morrison."

Sandy blushed, gave him a tender kiss, and laughed out loud in pure joy.

The wedding day dawned clear and bright. Richard was so anxious for the ceremony, that he got to the church hours in advance. He looked very handsome in his white dinner jacket, black tie, and black trousers. The stark white of the jacket made his eyes look an even deeper shade of blue. Though his hands were shaking, he managed to pin his boutonniere; a white rose, baby's breath, with a small bit of blue ribbon, on his jacket. But when the time came to walk out onto where the preacher was waiting, Richie was cool and calm.

Karen walked down first in a full skirted pale blue dress. The small hat perched precariously on her head was the same shade of blue and adorned with dark blue ribbons. She carried a small bouquet of white roses and blue delphiniums. Karen took her place, turned, and the music began to swell into the wedding march.

The church was full, but Richie never took his eyes from the spot where he would first see Sandy. His breath caught at his first vision of her. She wore a full long-sleeved gown that barely skimmed the top of her shoes. She had a short veil secured with a small tiara on top of her head. She also carried a bouquet of white roses and blue delphiniums but hers had long trailing dark blue ribbons. He saw her soft smile as their eyes met and if anyone could hear his heartbeat they would swear it was saying hurry, hurry.

Mr. Harrison kissed Sandy on the cheek and then placed her hand in Richie's. As their hands touched, there was that shot of electricity again and they both shot a knowing smile at each other.

The preacher spoke over them, but neither could later recall a word he said, they were so focused on each other. Someone cleared their throat to break the spell when the preacher declared them man and wife and they shared a kiss.

They seemed to float back down the aisle. Everyone followed them out of the church. Sandy kissed her parents and gave Richie's mother a quick hug. As the turned to get in the car, Sandy reached back and threw her bouquet. Karen was quick to grab it and gave the best man a wink.

As the couple drove off, tin cans bounced noisily behind the old Ford. Several people wiped a tear. Never had anyone witnessed a ceremony between such a loving couple.

The couple turned off onto Dragonfly Lane and Sandy became quiet. She suddenly become nervous. She turned and looked at this man that was now her husband and her heart slowed back down. After all, what was she nervous about? This was Richie, her soulmate, the love of her life.

Richie opened her car door, took her hand, and led her to the cottage door. He reached down and gently picked her up, opened the door, and walked through to their new life.

Richie and Sandy seemed to lead a magical life. Sandy kept house, cooked, and cleaned as most women did at that time. Richie got promoted at the factory and their life became very comfortable in the little cottage.

There were only a few times when Sandy noticed a concerned look pass across Richie's face. She worried that he was growing dissatisfied with his job and would upset their little life with a job change.

One evening, Richie came home from work and asked Sandy to sit down with him for a talk. Sandy's heart began to race. She feared their life was about to change and she was not ready for that. To her surprise, he wanted to talk about how things in the country were rapidly changing. President Johnson had pushed through a civil rights act to end discrimination against women and minorities and provide equal opportunities at work. Richie believed in equal rights, but he feared for his job. Factory work would probably be one of the first industries to be affected by equal rights.

The repetitive work he did at the factory, gave Richie plenty of time to reflect on his life. He realized he hadn't found that job to give his life meaning. He knew this kind of thinking upset Sandy, but he couldn't hold it in any longer.

"Sandy, I need to talk to you about my job. I don't feel like it's the right one for me anymore."

"But honey, you've done so well there. You got that promotion, didn't you? You are in charge of your whole department. Isn't that a good thing? Doesn't that make you feel fulfilled?" Sandy asked in desperation.

"It was a good thing and I'm proud of what I have accomplished but something just doesn't feel right with me. Maybe it's all the unrest within the country that is making me antsy, I don't know. I just know, there is something bigger I am meant to do. I have been thinking a lot about my father. You know, he loved this country so much that he gave up his life for it."

Sandy did not like where this conversation was going. She tried to change the subject. "Let's eat first, then we can talk. Supper is going to get cold."

"No, supper can wait. This can't. I know this may be a shock to you, but I want to follow in my father's footsteps. I want to serve my country like he did. I think that may be what's been missing from my life. A sense of purpose."

"But what about me? Doesn't our marriage give you a sense of purpose? I don't understand why you want to change our life when it's going so good?" She began to cry.

Richie took her in his arms and stroked her hair. "I'm sorry honey. Just forget what I said."

But Sandy couldn't forget. Now she knew that her husband was unhappy and that was the last thing she wanted for him. It was time for a lot of soul searching on her part and she wasn't looking forward to it.

A few months later, they were watching the news. It seemed everyone was protesting something these days. The war in Vietnam was going strong and people had very strong opinions one way or another. Sandy thought the issue of following in his father's footsteps had been forgotten. He had not brought it up since that one conversation and she hoped that was the end of it. But suddenly Richie tossed the TV Guide on the sofa.

"I just can't sit here anymore and do nothing, Sandy. I grow more restless every day. I want you to understand that it is not you. It doesn't have anything to do with you or our marriage. It's me. I feel that my dad fought and died for this country, yet all I do is manufacture car parts day in and day out. I feel like he would be ashamed of me and I can't stand it. Please tell me you understand, Sandy. Please say you can see how this is tearing me apart."

Sandy was still blinking back the tears at his remark 'it doesn't have anything to do with you'. How could he say that? Of course, it had everything to do with her. She shook her head to clear the tears from her eyes and looked at him.

"Richie, everything you decide has to do with me. We are two parts of a whole and your decisions affect me too. I understand your restlessness. The whole country is restless right now and of course, it spills over into everyone's lives. Maybe that's all it is. I feel restless sometimes too, like I should be getting out there and doing things. I get tired just doing housework. Maybe I want to do more than I am right now. What would you say to that?"

"I'd say I understand completely. Life is changing all around us, its natural that we would want to be a part of it. So, you understand why I want to enlist?"

Sandy's breath caught in her throat. "That's not what I meant! No, I don't want you to enlist!"

Richie looked disappointed at her outburst. He got up and walked outside. He stayed there until she went to bed. It was the first time they had let an argument go on past bedtime and Sandy was worried. She woke up at midnight and when he was still not in bed, she went to find him and apologize.

She found him sleeping like a baby on the sofa. It was all she could do not to shake him and make him continue their conversation. That feeling quickly passed and she could think of nothing but him enlisting. He would go away, far away and she sat down on the floor beside him and cried.

Richard must have sensed her presence and woke up. He pulled her onto the sofa beside him and wrapped his arms around her. They lay like that until the sun came up.

Sandy was wakened with soft kisses and she wrapped her arms around his neck. "I don't want to fight, Richie, really I don't. I just don't understand why you would want to leave me."

"It is not that I want to leave you honey. It's just that this pull, this urge, to stand up and fight for my country is so strong. I think it's been in me all along, I just didn't stand still long enough to recognize it. Please try to understand. I love you more than anything but I love my country too. I would not be the man you fell in love with if I didn't follow my conscience."

She took in a shaky breath. How could she argue with him, this devotion to what's right and true is what drew her to him in the first place? She didn't know how she would survive while he was gone, but she loved him too much to convince him to give up his beliefs.

She sat up and looked Richie right in those deep blue eyes. What she saw there was a sincere hope for understanding. She reached over and brought his hand up to her mouth for a kiss. "I can't say I like it, because I don't. I will worry every single second until you come back to me. But I do understand and respect your conviction. I love you and I will support your decision."

To prevent Sandy seeing the tears shining in his eyes, Richie took her into his arms. His love for her was almost too much to bear. It would be torture to be away from her, but his beliefs were too strong to resist.

Within the next month, Richie quit his job and made several trips to the recruitment office. He'd come home and tell Sandy a watered-down version of what had been discussed. As each day passed, Sandy became more anxious. All she really knew of the war was what she saw on the tiny black and white TV and what she overheard other people saying. Neither gave her a feeling of confidence.

The day they told her parents the news, they were met with arguments. Her mother cried and hugged them both, but her father shook his newspaper in front of Richie's face asking him if he even read it. Why would someone volunteer to go off to a war people were defecting to Canada to avoid? Why would he voluntarily leave his wife and a good job to go off and fight in some God-forsaken jungle? Could he be that naïve to think sacrificing his life would make a difference in the long run? Did he even realize what the war was about?

Richie calmly answered all the man's questions and protests as best he could. He made it clear that he would not be dissuaded. He had finally realized his purpose in life and was determined to follow where his belief lead him. He tried to explain how much he regretted leaving Sandy. They explained that she would continue living in the cottage, but he asked if they would help look after her while he was gone. Sandy sat with her eyes downcast. Afraid if she looked her parents in the eye, they would see her fear and remark on it to Richie. After much conversation for and against, neither side won their argument. They went home with nothing but a promise to look after Sandy and a prayer for safety to surround him.

The next weekend, the couple made the four-hour trip down highway 79 to Memphis. Richie felt the need to tell his mother face to face of his decision. He was not sure how she would take it and was glad Sandy was going with him. When his mother opened the door and saw them standing on her doorstep, her heart leapt with joy. She had been hoping that they would soon make her a grandmother and believed they had come in person to tell her the happy news. After looking closer at their faces, Mrs. Morrison's hope faded. She knew this was not what she had hoped for and she dreaded hearing what they had to tell her.

They all took a seat in the small living room and Richie drew a deep breath.

"Mom, you know I love you so much..." he began.

"Richard, just come out with it. I love you too and we can handle whatever you have to tell me."

"You know I have struggled for a long time to find my purpose in life. I have tried job after job and nothing seemed to satisfy that longing."

"I thought you were happy at the factory, son. What happened?"

Richard went over and sat on the arm of her chair and took his mom's hand in his. "Mom, I have wrestled with this decision for many weeks. I have discussed it with Sandy and she agrees with me. I have decided to honor dad and enlist in the Army. I feel so strongly that this is my destiny, to fight and protect my country. I wonder I hadn't figured it out long ago."

Mrs. Morrison broke out in sobs. "Richard, you can't. Oh, please don't do this. I couldn't bear to lose you too. Sandy, tell him not to go. Tell him you want him to stay home with you. Oh, Richard."

Sandy started crying and rushed over to take her other hand. "Oh, mom, I'm worried sick about him too but he asked for my support. I have to respect his decision even if I'm not entirely sure about it."

Richard wrapped his arms around the two women and let them cry. He hated that he had upset them so, but his conviction was just as strong as it had been.

After their sobs turned into whimpering hiccups, Richard released them and stood up.

"Can't you think about this a little longer, Richard? Pray about it before you make such a big decision," Mrs. Morrison pleaded.

"I've already signed all the paperwork. I report in two weeks for training. I don't know where I'll be stationed but I promise to write and keep you both informed as much as I can. I love you both so much and I hate that I have disappointed you but it is something I have to do. Please understand, Mom."

Resigned to the fact there was no changing his mind, Mrs. Morrison stood up, smoothed down her skirt, and excused herself to go in the kitchen to make coffee. She asked Sandy to please help her get the cups ready.

When both women were alone in the kitchen, Mrs. Morrison turned to Sandy and asked point blank if she had agreed to let Richard go to war.

Sandy had to answer truthfully. "While I am scared to death for his safety, I have to support my husband. He is so calm and sure of this, I just have to pray this is right for him. I know you are disappointed, mom, but he needs us to be strong. We'll lean on each other and we'll get through this."

They shared the coffee, had a quick supper, then turned in for the night. In the morning, when they got ready to leave, Mrs. Morrison hugged Sandy then Richard. She held on for a long time, saying a prayer asking God to watch over her boy. She held in her tears until they had pulled out of the driveway. Then she broke down.

The next two weeks passed by quickly. There were papers to fill out, ID cards to get issued, and long talks to be had. Richard drove Sandy out to the base to get familiar with the places she would need in the future. They went to the commissary and got her stocked up on groceries. They walked through the PX and bought anything he might need to take with him. He then had her practice her driving. He drove them around most of their marriage and he wanted to be sure she knew how to handle the old Ford.

She went along with anything he suggested, knowing he knew what was best for her, but Sandy's heart was breaking. The time to say goodbye was creeping up entirely too fast. The night before he was to report, she made his favorite supper and they lingered over dessert.

"I sure will miss your cooking, Sandy. You cook even better than my mom, did I ever tell you that? Please don't tell her though," he said laughing in an attempt to lighten the mood. "You have Mr. O'Shaunessy's number if anything goes wrong here at the house and your dad can help you keep the car running. I'll write you whenever I can. You write me back and they'll get the letters to me. If anything should happen, you have all those papers that we signed. Keep them in a safe place, okay?"

At that remark, Sandy let out a broken sob. "Oh, don't say such a thing, Richie. Promise you'll come back to me. Promise."

He went over and kissed the top of her head, whispering, "I promise sweetheart, I will always be with you."

They went to bed and held each other tight. No words were necessary. They just let their closeness convey their love and commitment to each other.

Dawn came all too quickly and he was gone.

The first month Richard was gone, Sandy spent her days wandering around the cottage. She cleaned and dusted though the house was spotless. She worked out in the garden, planting vegetables and nourishing the flowers that returned. She polished the windows until they shone. She took the Ford out and drove it up and down the driveway. She realized this was a pitiful attempt to keep her mind occupied, but it wasn't working. All she could think about was Richie.

He called her every week while at camp, but they were being transferred soon and he wouldn't be able to talk as often. Their correspondence would mostly consist of letters. He tried to describe his life at camp, making it sound like a grand adventure, but Sandy knew that was strictly for her benefit. A new friend took his picture outside his barracks and she had it framed and put on the mantle. Another picture was of him sitting on his cot, a framed picture of her beside him on his footlocker. That one she sat on her nightstand. She kissed it every night before bed and when she woke in the morning. She was trying, she really was, but it was so hard.

At first, his letters came somewhat regularly. He never said exactly where he was at the time. His letters mostly talked about her. He wrote how he missed her, her smile, and the way her eyes twinkled when she laughed. He asked questions about the garden and how their flowers were growing. He asked if everything was alright with the cottage and had she seen Mr. O'Shaunessy lately. Sandy loved the letters and treasured every word, but the time spent in between was torture. She tried to fill her time with knitting, gardening, learning new recipes, anything to keep herself busy. But the days weighed heavy.

Sandy had to find something to occupy her time until Richie came home, but what? Opportunities were hard to come by, especially for a woman. Women's lib was new and people were still accustomed to a woman's place being in the home. Sandy wasn't into protesting or burning her bra, but she did believe in equal rights. She felt Richie would agree with her. Every day, she would get the paper and pour over the employment ads. So many said a man was preferred. There were ones aimed more at women, such as the housekeeping jobs, but those didn't interest her. She had done all the dusting and cleaning she could stand these past few months and she wanted something with a little more excitement.

Her first job was sales clerk in the women's hat and hosiery department at McNeal's Ladies Shop. She unpacked the hats and hosiery and displayed them appealingly. Half her day was spent straightening up packages of hose and making sure they were in the correct drawer. This was incredibly boring. With the hats, she had an opportunity to use a little creativity as she helped ladies choose ones that matched their outfits.

Sandy told herself it was at least something to do, but that didn't help much. The more women's lib took hold, the less hose and hats were being worn. The clientele became more and more the older generation and she had less and less in common with them. She found herself longing for a life of bare legs, pixie cuts, and shorter skirts. Her boss sensed her dissatisfaction and offered to move her to dresses, but Sandy feared the boredom would be the same.

After writing a long letter to Richie explaining her dilemma, she decided to quit her job. She knew he would agree as he had not wanted her to work anyway. It was back to the help wanted ads for her. She found one for telephone operator that sounded appealing. Processing phone calls and forwarding them could be interesting. You would talk to different people all the time. She applied and soon was sitting in front of a large board with flashing lights, talking into a microphone, and wearing a little set of headphones.

Being an operator was more interesting than store clerk, but not by much. Some people would get chatty, but most were direct and straight to the point. Sandy felt herself grow bored again. Maybe she wasn't cut out to work. As Richie pointed out in his last letter, she didn't have to work. His Army pay was enough to take care of things right now. Couldn't he see that without him here, her life was not the same.

She didn't tell him about the war protests going on in town. She didn't tell him how people were so divided about the war, that she stopped saying her husband was over there fighting. If she happened to mention that he had volunteered, she was often met with harsh criticism and derisive remarks. Some people even quit associating with her at all. She told them she had not wanted him to go, but she did support his decision. It didn't matter.

She often worried how he and the other war veterans would be treated when they returned home. She hoped and prayed they would be treated as all those before them who had given much of their life for their country. But it didn't seem it would. Sandy quit reading the paper and watching TV due to the changed attitude of people. Some returning veterans were met with protesters shouting 'baby killer' and her heart ached for them and Richie. All this she kept in her heart, afraid to tell Richie how things were changing.

Her job was okay, but Sandy kept an eye on the employment ads hoping for something a little more challenging. Women's roles in the workplace were changing slowly and it was recognizable in the ads appearing recently. There were now jobs with words such as 'room for advancement' something unheard of previously. She wasn't exactly sure how far the that would go, but she was anxious to find out. One of the ads was for a typist and clerk for a real estate firm. Her typing skills were excellent, but since school, she had gotten a little rusty. She spent a few days on a typewriter at the public library honing her skills until she felt ready to apply.

Mr. Feltner, the head realtor at the firm, was a kindly older gentleman. He immediately liked Sandy and offered her the job. He respected that Sandy's husband had volunteered to serve as his own son had been drafted. For the first time in a long time, Sandy felt as if she could relax. She no longer had to make excuses or avoid the subject of the war. She could speak honestly with Mr. Feltner and felt no judgement, only understanding and sympathy.

Sandy loved her job. There was always something new to learn. The market was very busy with women buying their first home on their own. She loved these. The women were so excited and their faces glowed with their new-found independence. As Sandy typed up contracts, she learned a lot about the business. What she didn't understand, Mr. Feltner was eager to teach her. Their shared interest in the war forged a strong bond between the two. He gave Sandy more and more responsibility. Soon, she was running the office. The first thing she did was hire more women.

But if a man applying for a job was a returning vet, he immediately went to the front of the hiring list. Sandy and Mr. Feltner both had a soft spot for them.

Time practically sped by for Sandy though the war seemed to move slower and slower. Her letters from Richie became less frequent and much shorter. She could tell he was getting discouraged. She tried to fill her letters with light, humor, and love but felt much of it fell on deaf ears. She casually mentioned her job, but didn't go into a lot of details. She didn't want Richie to think her life was moving on without him though sometimes it felt like it was.

She tried to keep things the same as possible, but life was destined to be different. Her appearance had changed for one thing. She had finely given in and got a short, pixie cut that fell just below her ears. She wasn't sure if Richie would approve, so she didn't mention it in her letters. She also wore shorter, straighter skirts with her bare legs. She told herself it was just for convenience sake, but to be honest, she loved the feeling of freedom. Surely Richie would understand, but there was no sense bothering him with such small details until he came home.

Sandy felt guilty enjoying her life while Richie was over there fighting for his. At work, she could escape the worry for a small time. But at home, surrounded by reminders of their life together, loneliness and sadness took hold. Many times, she would cry herself to sleep clutching his picture to her chest. She spent extra time covering up the effects left from the night before, but Mr. Feltner could always tell. He would let her spend most of the day hidden behind a stack of paperwork.

It was another year without Richie. Mr. Feltner was so impressed with Sandy's knowledge and work ethic, he began letting her assist him in sales. She began showing the houses, especially those to women. People asked for her specifically. Mr. Feltner knew an opportunity when he saw one and encouraged Sandy to study for her real estate exam. With so much time on her hands each night, it was easy for her to read and memorize all the material. Mr. Feltner quizzed her as they rode to each open house and was pleased with her quick grasp of the market.

The morning in June of 1968 dawned hot and humid. Sandy was in a foul mood as she prepared for her day at the office. All her clothes felt hot and itchy. Nothing she tried felt cool. It must be the weather, she told herself. It's impossible to feel anything but grouchy when the day starts off this hot. As she fixed herself a cup of coffee, she heard the gravel begin to crunch as if a car was driving up. It couldn't be someone this early. Everyone knew she had to be at work before eight.

There was a sharp knock on the door. Sandy jumped. Suddenly her heart began to pound and she felt faint. No good news arrived on your doorstep this early in the morning. She stood frozen in the kitchen until the sharp knock rang out a second time. Slowly, as if her feet were in quicksand, she made her way to the door. Opening the door, Sandy saw a man wearing a uniform. She drew in her breath as she realized it was Western Union, but froze again when she saw the telegram held out to her. Backing up, Sandy refused to take it from him. She was still shaking her head no when he took her hand and gently placed the envelope in her palm. He muttered a quick 'I'm so sorry' as he backed out the door. Sandy sank to the floor with the envelope now clutched to her heart.

Everything was forgotten as images of Richie laughing and Richie smiling ran through her mind. She saw him standing before her, blue eyes twinkling as he said something to make her laugh. Oh, Richie, no, it can't be. Sandy slowly opened the envelope. The only words she could make out was 'We regret to inform you' and 'killed in action'. Her whole body began to shake and the telegram fell from her hand. This could not be true. She had just received a letter from him yesterday. He described the jungle as overlapping sheets of green and how the bugs were so thick you had to sweep a path through them with your hand. He couldn't be gone. It must be a mistake.

After eight, her phone started ringing but Sandy couldn't bring herself to answer it. After several hours with no word, Mr.

Feltner became concerned and drove out to the little cottage. The door was open and entering, he saw Sandy still sitting on the floor with the dreaded telegram beside her. He rushed over to help her to a chair and went to the kitchen to start a pot of tea. He wasn't sure why, but his wife always made tea when something happened, so he did too. When it was ready, he took a cup and placed it beside Sandy. He reached over and began to pat her on the shoulder, unsure of what else to do. Sandy, who had seemed almost catatonic, broke out in heart wrenching sobs. All he could make out was 'he's gone, he's gone and I didn't get to say goodbye.'

It was weeks before Richie's body could be shipped back home. Weeks of mourning for Sandy and his mother. Sandy's parents were no help as they persisted in saying he shouldn't have been there in the first place, he should have stayed home where he belonged.

Mr. Feltner was a great help. He assisted her in making the decisions that never seemed to end. Richie would receive a burial with full military honors but that did not comfort Sandy.

When the funeral procession left the base, protesters with signs lined the street and it took all Sandy's strength not to yell at them. How could they be so heartless and unfeeling? What if it was one of their loved ones?

At the cemetery, the preacher spoke his words of comfort and quoted Richie's favorite Bible verse, John 15:13, "Greater love hath no man than this, to lay down his life for his friends." At this, Mrs. Morrison and Sandy broke into sobs. They continued to cry while the flag was folded and presented and again during the gun salute. Slowly everyone began to leave, but Sandy could not bring herself to go. This would be the last time she would be near him. The last time she could reach out and touch him. How could she turn and leave? Mr. Feltner and Richie's mom came and took her arm in theirs and lead her to the car.

Life as Sandy knew it had ended. A new life alone had begun and she did not know what to do. She spent her days curled up in Richie's chair, cuddling his shirt in her arms. She struggled to smell his scent in his clothes. Nights were spent in bed, holding his picture, and crying uncontrollably. Mrs. Morrison stayed as long as she could, helping out around the house, and trying to console Sandy even though her own heart was broken. But eventually, life in Memphis with its responsibilities called and she had to go home.

The little cottage that had once felt so warm and comforting suddenly felt cold. The sunlight that came through the large windows was now harsh. The silence once soothing, now felt mocking. The little garden fell in ruin as Sandy could not muster up the energy to care for it. After several months, she phoned Mr. Feltner and said she wanted, no needed to find another place to live. The memories once shared in the little house were now too painful for her to bear. Mr. Feltner contacted Mr. O'Shaunessy and explained the situation.

Mr. Feltner persuaded Sandy to come with him to look at houses. He had lined up three that he felt would be good for her, but one he felt would be perfect to begin anew. He picked her up and was stunned at her appearance. She had the look of a frail waif, a homeless child unclaimed by anyone who cared. He took her hand as if she might break at any moment and seated her carefully in his car. Driving slowly down the bumpy drive, he tried to break the silence by describing the three houses. Sandy showed very little interest.

The first house was in a subdivision. While the house was nice, the neighbors seemed to be close enough to pass a cup of sugar back and forth without leaving your house. Sandy just shook her head. They moved on to the second one. It was a two-story model with lots of room. All Sandy could see was how empty the place seemed to be and how the rooms echoed with silence. Mr. Feltner began to lose hope that even this third house would not win her approval.

He pulled up a short, tree lined driveway to a tiny house, even smaller than her cottage. It was covered with beige wooden siding and had a cedar shingled roof. It looked like a tiny dollhouse complete with a red door and black shutters. Sandy let out a sound of delight as they pulled closer. Mr. Feltner smiled. His instinct had been right after all.

As they walked through the tiny house, Sandy could feel her spirits lift. She felt she could begin her new life here. Not forgetting Richie, for that could never happen. But carrying her memories and the best of him into a life here. As she walked through the rooms, she began to picture their things there and it felt comforting. She turned to Mr. Feltner with a smile on her face, the first one in months, and said "I'll take it."

Janet

The 1970s

Janet was desperate to find a place to rent. Her divorce was final today and she had been given thirty days to vacate the house. The house that had been her home for the past twenty years. She had no idea where to go, even where to start. How do you pack up your past in a few boxes? How do you choose what to keep and what to give away? Life was not fair. At least her life wasn't.

She shrugged her shoulders and headed into the dining room to start wrapping the china received as a wedding gift. As she lovingly smoothed the newspaper over the back of a plate, she spotted an ad in the rental section. Small Cottage-For Rent-Call 555-9487 for appointment to view. Small cottage, how small could it be? She was already downsizing from a 3000 sq. ft. home. Just how much more was she expected to give up? Janet picked up another plate to wrap. Suddenly her hands began to shake and she watched the plate fall to the floor as if in slow motion. It shattered into a thousand pieces, just like her life. Janet sat down in the floor and cried.

She allowed herself about thirty minutes to grieve, it was all she would give him today. He didn't even deserve that, the rat. How dare Frank take up with a younger woman and divorce her? Hadn't she given him the best years of her life? Now look where it had gotten her, forty-eight years old and starting over. How does she even begin to do that? She felt like she was defective. Traded in for a better model. Traded in like an old used car. One with over a hundred thousand miles and worn out tires. What a lovely picture. She shook her head as if to remove the image. She wasn't worn out, she was the very image of a mature woman who knew her worth. At least that's what she told herself, though the divorce settlement sure didn't prove that theory.

She had picked the best lawyer in town. In fact, he actually lived up the street from them and had attended many of their dinner parties. She considered him a friend and believed he would do what was best for her. How wrong she was! She hadn't considered while he may have been her friend, he was also her husband's and boys do stick together. Frank picked the lawyer nicknamed 'the barracuda' for his representative and how he lived up to that name.

It seemed to her that the 'good old boy network' conspired together to get her a pitiful settlement. She had one month to vacate the house, their home, the one she had designed and decorated. She was to receive a mere pittance in alimony. This was to last two years, giving her enough time to find a job. That was a whole other thing. The only job she had done in the past twenty years was president of the Garden Club and the Home Demonstration Club. Those came with prestige yes, but did not qualify her for a job in the real world. Not that either the lawyers or her now ex-husband cared.

Okay, enough. She had too much to do to relive that whole fiasco. Now was the time to pull up her big girl panties and get on with her life.

She stood up and began to pack again. As she ran her hands over another plate, memories of their first dinner in the house, that Thanksgiving when she burnt the turkey, and the Christmas dinners they hosted, drifted in a loop through her mind. When had it all gone wrong? When had he decided he wanted someone else? The plate slipped out of her hand. Oops! This crash felt better somehow. She picked up another plate, and let it go, on purpose this time. Crash! Looking down at the shards of china, Janet knew she should be devastated, but wasn't. She picked up a handful of salad plates and let them slowly slip through her grasp one by one. The china fragments started to pile up. Good! Janet slowly took up another piece and dropped it on the floor. She looked at the mess and saw her life represented by the fragments.

She paused one second to set aside two plates, two cups, and two saucers; just enough for use in her new place. The rest of the set found its way to the floor and she felt exceedingly euphoric. Reaching into the cabinet, she got out the crystal and smashed it one fancy stemmed glass at a time.

Finally finished with the dining room, she moved to the kitchen. There she found two old jelly glasses in the back of the cabinet, leftover from her country phase and she carefully wrapped them and set them in the box. Filling another box with some of her pots and pans completed the kitchen. She reached for the broom to sweep up the glass in the dining room. She suddenly stopped and set the broom with the boxes going with her. No, not this time Frank. This time, for once, you can clean up the mess yourself.

That evening, Janet called the number in the cottage ad. It was answered by an older sounding man with an unrecognizable accent. She explained her interest in seeing the cottage and the man said he would meet her at ten tomorrow morning and gave her the address, One Dragonfly Lane.

There weren't many cars out on the road, it was a Sunday after all, and most people were in church. Janet didn't expect to have trouble finding the cottage, but the man's directions were a little confusing. She passed by the turn twice before finally seeing the small street sign. It was almost entirely obscured by vines. There were no other houses on the street and the tiny lane led straight to the front of the cottage. And a cottage it was. It couldn't be bigger than the garage of her current home. Simple, red brick, and a green door. Nothing fancy. Janet took a few minutes to take it all in before going to the door and ringing the bell.

Mr. O'Shaunessy was his name, but he said to call him Charles. He showed her the whole of the house in less than five minutes. It consisted of a kitchen with a small table that let down off the wall, a bedroom, bathroom, and a tiny sitting room. Certainly, different from what she was used to, but somehow, the coziness of it all appealed to her. Maybe she could go to some flea markets and find some treasures to add to what was already there. That way she wouldn't have to bring any of her old life with her. For the first time in a long time, she felt a faint stirring of excitement. Janet turned to Mr. O'Shaunessy and said "I'll take it!"

Janet drove back to her house, relieved that one problem had been solved. She had a place to live. Small though it was, it somehow promised a peace that had been lacking in her life these past few months.

The next day, Janet continued to pack. There was not much in the living room that she would be taking with her. It was all way too fancy for the little cottage and carried too many memories of the parties held there. She was sad to leave her beloved piano behind, but the little house was too small to hold it and still fit in anything else. She took down the portraits of her parents that were framed in antique oval frames. These would look right at home, more comfortable in the cottage than they had been in the pretentious display Frank had wanted. There, living room done. On to the den.

The den, that masculine room he had demanded to show off his manly skills. He had never killed a deer in his life, but there were multiple deer heads stuffed and mounted on the walls. She had grown sick listening to him brag about his 'hunting' conquests. Everything in this room was done in dark shades. Yes, she had decorated it, but done so to his specifications. The red and black plaid sofa now made her want to throw up, but instead she discreetly punched a few small holes in the seat cushions. Childish, she knew, but she did it anyway. There was absolutely nothing in here she wanted. He could keep it all.

Janet was in the zone and didn't want to stop packing but she was starved. She looked in the fridge and found some leftover chicken, a tomato, and a diet cola. Not bad for an impromptu lunch. She put her finds on one of the packed boxes and sat down in the floor for a kind of picnic. Something Frank hated. He hated the grass, the bugs, and the lack of elegance. Looking back now, Frank hated a lot of things that she liked. She had adjusted her life around his for so long. It might be fun to do some things she enjoyed for a change. She finished her drink and made a mental list of things she might like to try.

Still musing over the many fun things that had been lacking in her life, Janet went back to work. In the bedroom, she opened her jewelry box and ran her hand over all the rings, bracelets, and necklaces Frank had gifted her over the years. She picked up the box, tempted to dump them all in the trash, but then set it back down. She put up with a lot to get these. In fact, she could say she had earned them putting up with all his nonsense for the past thirty years. She closed the box and put it into one of the boxes. Then she cushioned it with the needlepoint throw pillows she had so painstakingly made. They would look so good in the cottage, give it a nice homey feel. She made a mental note to pick up new bed pillows and sheets along with groceries.

She dragged a large box over to the walk-in closet. Oh, she had loved this luxury. She hadn't looked at the size of the closet in the cottage, but assuming how small the whole place was, it had to be tiny. Time to go through her clothes and get rid of anything unneeded in her new life. Janet started pulling out her evening clothes. Her first instinct was to grab a pair of scissors and slice them into ribbons, but no, maybe someone, somewhere could get use out of them. So, she grabbed another box and started a donate pile. She threw in the shoes and purses that matched the dresses. The next items were her part of their matching outfits. It made her sick to think of them both dressing alike, matching sweaters, shirts, and jackets. Ugh! They definitely had to go. She was embarrassed that she had been so 'in love' as to dress alike.

The first box quickly filled with the rest of her clothes. She did pare down the number of jeans, shoes, blouses, and sweaters she kept. Who needed fifteen pair of jeans and twenty some odd sweaters anyway? It actually felt good to see the donate pile grow.

In a smaller box, Janet carefully put in her large collection of makeup and colognes. She did dearly love them all, but her signature scent was White Shoulders. Frank gifted her with the whole set every Christmas. Well, she'd better make this bit last, because it would not be in her budget going forward.

She packed her books next, careful not to pack them too heavy. She had always loved to read and had many of her beloved childhood books. Little Women was placed side by side with the latest from Phyllis Whitney and Steven King.

She stood in the center of the bedroom and turned around slowly. She looked at everything and memories came flooding back of Frank fastening the pearls around her neck. Her straightening his tie. Them both staying up late watching old movies on the TV. Janet allowed one tear to slip down her cheek before she angrily wiped it away. No! She would not cry! He did not deserve it.

Turning to the bathroom, she grabbed another box. First, she took all the towels. They were the luxurious fancy hotel ones she had splurged on and she was taking them all. Then she put in all the shampoo, soaps, lotions, and anything else she found. She went to get another box for all the cleaning supplies. No reason for her to have to buy everything new. Let him do it. As she mentally went over everything, she spotted their toothbrushes hanging side by side. How intimate is that small thing? Hmmm, she got an evil idea. Should she? He'd never know if she used his to clean the toilet, would he? He did deserve it. Hmmm.

Fitting as many boxes as she could into her Cadillac, she headed out to the cottage. There was still plenty of daylight left, so she ran by Walmart and picked up new bedding and some groceries.

Janet took a deep breath of the earthy scent along the lane leading up to the house. She looked up through the leafy green canopy and marveled at the beams of late sunlight coming through. She felt her soul being refreshed and renewed. It was a start.

Making another trip back to the old house, she packed up what boxes were left into the trunk and back seat of the car. She made one last trip through the rooms, saying her goodbyes. She did cry then. She cried for the good times and she had to admit that there had been some. She cried for these last few months and the utter betrayal she felt. She cried for what could have been. Then she drew herself up, straightened her shoulders, took a deep breath, and stepped out the door.

Janet's first morning in the cottage dawned sunny and bright. She made herself a cup of coffee and took it out on the patio to enjoy before setting up the house. She admired the butterflies that fluttered around the flower bed and laughed at the antics of a squirrel who poked his head out of the brush. Her heart felt lighter than it had in a long time. She was actually looking forward to putting her things out. She loved decorating but Frank liked things to stay a certain way. She shook her head, she didn't have to worry about what he liked and didn't like anymore.

She started with the little sitting room, placing her needlepoint pillows on the sofa and chairs. She set out some treasured pieces of glassware she inherited from her grandma. She filled one of the vases with flowers cut from the garden. The only thing missing was her piano. But as she turned around, she felt a great satisfaction at its homey feeling.

Next was the kitchen. She hung up her copper pots and pans and laughed as they caught the light from the window and shot beams around the room. It didn't take very long to put up the little china she had brought. She scrubbed out the sink, wiped off the cabinets, and was done.

There wasn't much left to do in the bedroom as she had done most of it last night. She made up her bed, fluffed the pillow, and opened the window to let in some fresh air. She hung her lone toothbrush up in the bathroom and put away the linens. Well, that hadn't taken too long. She walked through the rooms and admired her handiwork. She made a mental list of anything she had forgotten at the store and what she'd look for at the next flea market.

It wasn't even twelve o'clock, so she grabbed a book and went back out to the patio. The sun was so warm, she soon fell asleep.

She must have been exhausted. When she woke up, she had missed lunch and was famished. She fixed a small salad and took it back outside to eat. She stayed long enough to watch the stars come out and the moon light up the back yard. She listened to the crickets and katydids sing, something she hadn't really heard since she was a kid.

When the mosquitos got bad, she went into the house, grabbed a pen and paper and settled into the sofa. A thought had come to her. What if she did all the things she had not had a chance to as a teen? Marrying Frank had put a stop to all the silly things teens get to experience.

She wrote down roller skating, that sounded like fun and how hard could it be? She had owned a pair of clip on roller skates when she was little. It should be easy to pick back up. Now, what else? Disco? It was the 'thing' right now and looked like fun when she watched it on Dance Fever. The list looked too small, surely there was more she had missed out on? Bowling would be fun. She'd need to practice first before joining a league. Satisfied she had a good start on her list, she went to bed.

Janet spent the next few weeks getting settled into a routine. Coffee in the garden each morning, then looking at employment ads and dismissing them was next. Lunch and an afternoon nap followed. Sometimes she went to the movies, but didn't like sitting alone. There was no one to share exciting scenes with. No one's arm to grab during the scary scenes in Jaws. She tried spending time at the arcade in the mall, but she wasn't any good at Space Invaders or Asteroids and it cost too much money. She definitely needed to find something else to occupy her time.

Maybe she should go out and find a job. She was going to need one eventually, so why not try it out now? She started looking at employment ads in the newspaper. There wasn't much she knew how to do, so it needed to be easy. It took her a whole week to find something even remotely doable for her, a waitress. How hard could that be? She'd been serving food all her life. Monday, she went down to the diner on Main Street promptly at nine to apply. They asked a lot of questions and Janet must have answered them correctly, because she was told to be there tomorrow morning at five for training and to start her shift.

At four thirty, Janet barely had her eyes open but managed to pull herself out of bed, get dressed, and get to work a minute before five. The manager frowned and tapped her watch. Janet vowed to do better tomorrow.

Janet was given a light blue uniform and a name tag with Betty's name crossed out and her name written over it in thick black ink. The red and white apron had a few grease stains but was relatively clean. She was excited to start earning her way in the world.

She followed the manager around as she started coffee and waited on a few of the regulars. Janet wrote down their orders as the manager repeated them for her, then went to the kitchen to leave them with the cook. The cook gave a mock salute as she was introduced to him, then went right back to work. After following along with the manager for a few more tables, the restaurant got busy and Janet was left on her own.

Her hand shook as she poured the first table's coffee. She spilt drinks at the second table. Gave coffee to the third table when they hadn't wanted any. Rough start, but things were bound to get better. It took her so long to take the orders, that she had to repeat the coffee before they got their food. She forgot to check back at the kitchen and the first table's food was cold when she served it. She got the second and third tables orders mixed up. The cook had to make all three tables food again and he was furious. The manager shot daggers her way and went to apologize to Janet's tables. Serving food had never been this hard before.

Things did not improve much by quitting time. Janet's shoulders and feet were aching. Her hair was sticking out all over her head and her apron had turned itself around. The manager told her not to come back. But taking pity on her, told her to try the Dairy Dip as they were looking for someone.

Janet could barely move when her alarm went off. She hurt all over. Did she really have to have a job?

Determined to prove she could do something right, she went to apply at the drive in. The manager said he would give her a chance, even with no experience, she was better than nothing.

The next day, she pulled on the Dip's uniform and apron and arrived early at ten minutes to eleven. The manager explained the drive-up process. She would talk to the customers through a speaker/microphone and take their orders. After dropping off their orders to the cook, she would fill the drinks, get the ketchup and mustard, and prepare the tray. Once the order was ready, she would take the tray out to the correct stall and collect the money.

Cars started pulling into stalls faster than she could take the orders back to the kitchen. When she finally got a break, she had five orders in her hand. The cook shook his spatula at her as she quickly turned and left. In her nervousness, she overfilled all the drinks and had to wipe down the trays. Her speaker kept sounding off with demands for food and Janet broke down in tears. Why had she thought this would be easier? She didn't have the mental fortitude to be a waitress. She finished her shift in a haze of complaints. She went home and fell into bed, a sticky mess from all the cola she had spilt on herself. She was too tired to care.

She got to work the next morning thirty minutes early with her uniform and apron in hand. She found the manager, handed them in and thanked him for the opportunity. The manager accepted the items, a look of relief on his face.

Two days wasted, Janet thought, but lesson learned. She was not cut out to be a waitress. She would have to look for something else, something easier.

After a few days, Janet felt like herself again. What should she do now? The days stretched out one just like the other. At least when she was married, she had something to do. Frank always had some errand for her to run, dry cleaning to deliver, or laundry to do. Heaven forbid he wore the same suit twice in one week.

Watching TV and soap operas became her daily entertainment. The Young and the Restless and All My Children were the highlight of her days. Shows like The Walton's and Mash filled her nights. Saturday cartoons had never interested her, so she spent her mornings in the garden with her coffee. But afternoon found her in front of the TV watching American Bandstand. Disco fascinated her and was something she thought she would enjoy.

Disco was so lively and it looked fairly easy. Janet practiced in front of the TV each Saturday afternoon until she felt confident enough to go to a disco club. She went through her meager closet and found one silky dress she had saved. She cut the bottom into a handkerchief hem, very trendy, and loosened the top to fit down on her shoulders. When she tried it on, she felt very disco-y. She looked in the phone book and picked the disco with the catchiest name, Music Mania, perfect. She put on her reconstructed dress, heels, and sprayed her hair within an inch of its life. She was ready.

Finding a disco station on the car radio, she headed out. Seeing a bunch of twenty-year old's waiting at the door of the disco made her pause, but she had practiced too hard to back down now. She got some odd stares as she waited in line to pay, but she didn't care. The inside was decked out in spotlights and disco balls. Light danced off all the surfaces and it took her a minute to get her bearings. People pushed past her in a hurry to get to the dancefloor.

Janet found a seat back near the wall and waited for a song to come on that she knew. As she watched everyone else, she realized the dancing ranged from freestyle to line dancing. She had never been good at just getting up and dancing, but line dancing with its structure was more her style. Finally, her song came on and she made her way to the dancefloor to dance the electric slide. This was her time to shine. The beat pounded and the floor shook. Everyone lined up side by side and began the back and forth steps. She worked her way into the lineup and tried to get in step with the other dancers.

It proved harder than it seemed in her living room. She hadn't worn heels when practicing and this added a level of difficulty she had not anticipated. Only a few steps and shuffles in, Janet's ankle turned sideways, then her shoe fell off and scuttled across the floor. She tried to continue but stumbled and fell into the person next to her. Who fell into the next person and so on down the line.

The music continued thumping as she hobbled across the floor to pick up her shoe and head back to her table.

She sat and tried to gather up courage to leave. The mirrored disco ball lights were making her eyes water and the thumping of the music seemed to match the thumping in her head. She had to get out of there. This had been a miserable experiment. Was she too old for this single life she now found herself in?

The next week, she decided she really needed a job. Not for the money, but for the boredom. You can only clean your house so much and the little cottage wasn't that big after all. So, the job search began again.

While in line at the grocery, she overheard someone mention a job opening at a nearby photo shop. She loved taking pictures so it sounded like something she might enjoy. The next day, she went down to the shop and applied. She didn't have much work history, so she really had to sell her abilities. But the owner liked her and before she knew it, she was hired.

She arrived at work the next day bright and early. But apparently, she had misunderstood where she would be working. It seemed she would be working at a Photo Stop. A small building set in the parking lot of a store. It was a like a drive thru for photos. People would pull up, drop off their film, and then come back a few days later to pick them up. Janet would be responsible for labeling the envelopes, sending off the film, and taking payment when they were picked up.

At first, she was nervous and worried about making a mistake. But luckily, she was in the little building all by herself. There was no one looking over her shoulder. Even better, she had a TV and a refrigerator. What more did she need? Well, a bathroom would have been nice, but oh well. Beggars can't be choosers.

As the days went on, Janet became comfortable in her little cubicle. She even brought some plants and knick-knacks to make it homier. She definitely felt she had found her niche. One of the perks of the job was getting to look at everyone's photos. She told herself it was quality control. Really it was her fascination with how these other people lived. Most of the photos were people laughing and smiling. Sometimes, just sometimes, she was jealous. Here they were going about their lives while she was stuck. She didn't know how to move on. How do you move on from a marriage you thought would last forever? How do you let go of all the dreams? How do you move past feeling you weren't good enough?

The job helped take up her days, but she still had those long, lonely nights to get through. Disco was not her thing, that was evident. But what was? What could she do at night or on the weekends to make the time pass? She couldn't write, couldn't paint, and didn't know how to macramé. She didn't like going to movies alone and learning arcade games was too expensive when you were bad at it.

Suddenly, she remembered her list. Bowling. Frank belonged to a bowling league that he went to every Thursday night. Of course, he had his own ball with his initials on it, but she didn't need anything so fancy to start with. She would learn to bowl first, then get good enough to join a league. She went to bed with a smile on her face, looking forward to the weekend for a change.

Saturday afternoon, Janet looked up the nearest bowling alley. She had a good feeling about this, even the listing made it look like fun. She watched a few people line up and throw the ball down the lane. They certainly made it look easy. Picking a lane, she went to pick out a ball. There were so many, how did you choose the right one? She quickly realized that a lot of them were too heavy for her to lift, let alone throw down the lane. She finally found one light weight enough, and what fun, it was a pretty shade of pink. It was meant to be.

After watching everyone a few more times, she walked to the line and threw the ball down the lane. It rolled about three feet, then went into the gutter. Oh well, now what? By the time she had turned around, her ball was back. She picked it up and tried again. Gutter ball. She was discouraged but not deterred. She was determined to get this right.

There was a big group coming in, a bunch of kids and a couple of adults. They would be fun to watch. They couldn't all be pros, could they? They took up several lanes and eventually the one beside her was occupied. She nodded hello, then went back to practice, determined to not allow anything break her concentration. Gutter ball followed gutter ball.

Determined to get at least one ball down the lane, she gave the next throw a big toss. Horrified, she watched her bright pink ball go sailing into the next lane. How embarrassing! The kids next to her broke out into raucous laughter. Janet's felt her cheeks grow bright red. Another failure.

She had begun to gather her things, when one of the men from the group came over and stood beside her.

"Hello. I'm Pastor Thomas. I hope this rowdy group of kids is not throwing off your game. They do get pretty loud."

"Oh, no. They're not bothering me. I'm afraid I'm just that bad. This is my first-time bowling, but I bet you'd never have guessed that."

"Oh no," he smiled. "I would never have guessed. I'd be happy to give you some pointers if you don't mind. I'm not a pro by any means, but I've been coming with this church group for quite a while and picked up a few things."

"I sure would appreciate it Pastor, uh, Thomas?"

"Please just call me Thomas," he said as he reached over to pick up his own ball. "Let me give you a few pointers and I bet you'll get the hang of it in no time."

He stood beside her at the line and guided her arm and told her when to let go. To Janet's surprise, her ball rolled slowly down the lane and knocked over a pin. She let a yell in surprise and grabbed Thomas's arm. They both looked down at her hand and Janet removed it with a slight embarrassed laugh.

"Well, I think I've got the hang of it now. Thank you so much. I really appreciate your help."

"No problem. It was nice to meet you and good luck," he said as he stepped back over to his side of the lane.

Janet could hear the good-natured teasing he endured from the kids and her cheeks blushed again. She practiced a few more times and was pleasantly surprised when she knocked down a couple more pins. Pleased with her success, she gathered her things, nodded bye to the group of church goers and left. All in all, it had been a good afternoon.

Weeks went by with a new routine. Every Saturday she went to the bowling alley to practice, but she never saw the church group or Pastor Thomas again. Surprisingly, she was disappointed. Not that she was looking for a relationship, but it was nice to talk to someone. She was pleased to note that she had not forgotten how.

Work was going well. Bowling was going well. She decided to try another hobby. She couldn't just work and bowl for the rest of her life. She felt she needed something else. She saw a show about roller disco that looked fun. But no, disco was off the table. However, roller skating, that might be fun.

The next Saturday, Janet put on her favorite jeans, the ones she had to lay on the bed to get zipped, a loose-fitting t-shirt, and off she went to her next adventure. The parking lot was nearly empty, thank goodness. Less people to watch her hone her skating skills.

As she entered the rink, she was met with a wall of sound. People were laughing and yelling back and forth to each other. There was also the pounding of rubber meeting the wooden floor of the rink. It was overwhelming at first, but eventually it just dissolved into background noise. After paying, Janet went to pick out her skates. Her jeans were so tight, she could barely breathe as she bent over to tie them. Mental note, wear something looser next time. If there was a next time.

Standing up, Janet walked stiff legged over to the railing that circled the rink. She watched the other skaters as they flowed along, some going backwards, some dancing in rhythm to the music playing. Okay, time to quit watching and get out there. When the path was clear, she pushed herself off the rail and stepped out onto the floor.

She scrambled to keep her feet under her as they immediately took on a life of their own. She quickly reached back and grabbed the railing. Maybe she was a little too ambitious. She could just skate around holding on to the railing until she got the hang of it. Nobody would even notice. Around and round she went, the only problem when the railing ended to let the skaters enter and exit the rink. At those times, she said a silent prayer as she pushed off, hoping to reach the next railing without falling.

After making several rounds, Janet decided enough was enough and went for it. She let go and entered the circle of skaters. She had rolled forward a few feet when she lost her balance. As she felt herself falling, she flailed out with her arms trying to grab something to steady her. She managed to grab hold of someone and as she turned to apologize and thank them, her eyes met a familiar face. It was Pastor Thomas. Now her embarrassment was complete.

"Well, hello again," he said with a smile. "Fancy meeting you here. Are you trying out another hobby?"

Janet quickly let go of the claw like grip she had on his arm, but reached out when she felt herself falling again. This time, she did fall and managed to take him down with her. Oh, how mortifying. They seem to be all tangled arms and legs and as she scrambled around. He stood up quickly and reached out to pull her up.

As she stood, she realized she had twisted her ankle and couldn't put any weight on it. She didn't want to look any more pitiful than she already did, so she didn't say anything. She just bit down on her lip and tried not to limp. Holding her by the elbow, he guided her to a bench to sit down and catch her breath. He noticed her limp.

"Did you hurt yourself?" he asked as he helped her down.

"Oh no, I'm fine. Don't worry yourself."

"It's no worry at all. If you don't mind, I'll just sit with you a minute until you catch your breath. Would you like something to drink? I'd be happy to get you something."

"No, don't trouble yourself. You've done so much already. I don't know how I would have stood up, let alone get off the floor if you hadn't been there to help me. I'm afraid I've taken up too much of your time."

"Oh, I was happy to help. You're actually doing me a favor. I've been here for hours with my church kids and they're wearing me out. I'm grateful for the opportunity to sit down for a minute. By the way, I didn't catch your name last time we met."

"I'm Janet, Janet Johnson."

"Nice to formally meet you Mrs. Johnson," he asked with a question in his voice.

"I am the former Mrs. Johnson, so please call me Janet. Your church does a lot with the kids, don't they? I think that's great."

"Yes, we do a lot with the kids. They are fun to be with and I love to encourage them to attend church each week. They are such an integral part of the congregation."

"What's the name of the church you pastor?" she asked.

"It's Riverfront Baptist Church, over on Maple Street. I've been pastor there for the past three years and I love it. The congregation is very welcoming, friendly, and loving. It's been a really good fit for me."

"That's wonderful. I've heard good things about that church."

Thomas's face beamed. She could tell how much his church meant to him and it was endearing.

Endearing? What was she thinking? He was a pastor after all.

"Thank you, Janet. It's been nice talking to you and I'd love to continue our conversation. But I'd better get back to my kids before they get too rowdy. Can I walk you out to your car?"

"Oh no, I'll be fine. Thank you so much for your help and I really enjoyed talking to you too."

"Would you like to meet for coffee next Saturday morning? I usually go to the diner around eight and I'd love to continue our talk."

Janet hesitated. Was he asking her on a date? No, don't be silly. It was just coffee. No big deal.

"That sounds good," she found herself answering.

Thomas, a small grin on his face, said, "I'll see you there then. Oops, I see some sort of altercation starting between two of the boys. I better get over there. Bye, Janet."

"Bye, Thomas," she said as he quickly skated away.

Janet managed to limp her way to the car, but her mind wasn't on her ankle. She found herself thinking about Thomas and how deep and soulful his eyes were.

That next Saturday, Janet was very careful to dress more appropriately. She arrived promptly at eight and saw Thomas wave a greeting as he rose from his seat. She couldn't help but notice how nice he looked in his button-down shirt and jeans. What? Where did that come from? Stop it, Janet. He's a preacher. But she had noticed last time that he didn't wear a wedding ring.

Janet and Thomas met every Saturday morning for the next month and shared a cup of coffee. Janet told him about her divorce and how hard it had been starting a new, different life. Soon, she had told him about her first disastrous attempt at a job and the disco dancing fiasco. She loved the way his eyes crinkled when he laughed. He laughed with her, not at her, and that was a new thing for Janet. She found she liked a lot about him.

Thomas also began to share his life with her. He told her how he had married his college sweetheart right after graduation. He told her of the lean years when he was searching for the right church and what a wonderful preacher's wife she had been. His eyes filled with tears as he told her about the cancer that had taken her when she had just turned forty. That was when he had floundered in his faith. He spent several years away from the church, talking to God and dealing with his grief. It was only a few years ago he had come back to preaching and had moved here to Riverfront Church. He told how his faith, his church, and the people there had saved him.

Soon, Thomas invited her to his church. It had been so many years since she had stepped foot inside one she was nervous. Frank hadn't liked to go to church, so they hadn't gone. Despite her nerves, she found she was excited about to hear Thomas preach. He was changing so many wrong thoughts she had always believed and she wanted to hear more.

Janet dressed very carefully. She wanted to look nice and fit in with the rest of the congregation. When she arrived, she saw

Thomas at the front door greeting everyone and her nervousness disappeared. He looked up with a big smile on his face as she approached. He shook her hand and welcomed her, introducing her to the others standing there. Everyone was so welcoming. Janet took a seat midway but with a good view of the pulpit. Thomas's sermon was Luke 15, the prodigal son and she wondered if he had chosen it for her. She felt like she was returning home to something that had been missing from her life for far too long.

Once she told Thomas how she had left her beloved piano behind, he invited her to play the piano and accompany the organist at the church. Janet was thrilled. It solidified her feeling of belonging and everyone began to accept her as a treasured member of the church.

Janet's life took on a new routine again. Work during the week, she loved her job and some of the customers had become good friends. Saturdays were spent with Thomas. They would meet for coffee and then she went with him to help out on the excursions with the kids. She was bowling as well as everyone else. She'd even got a strike last time. It had been months since she had lane jumped and she was pretty proud of herself. She even saved up her money and got her own ball and bag.

With Thomas's patient teaching, she had learned to skate too. They could even couple skate as long as she didn't go backwards. The kids laughed and teased them but she knew now that it was all in good fun. Janet attended church every Sunday and even on Wednesday nights. She was learning so much and wondered why it had taken her so long to come back. She felt like she was part of a family again.

She had finally caught on to Thomas's hints and invited him to her house for a home cooked meal after church. She was a little nervous, it had been so long since she had cooked for anyone other than herself. But it turned out just fine. So fine in fact, that it soon turned into a Sunday ritual. After the meal, they would watch TV or go for a walk down the lane. Their favorite activity was to sit out on the patio, enjoying a glass of tea and a deep conversation. Janet felt like she had known Thomas her whole life and he felt the same.

One fall day, as they sat in the garden, Thomas cleared his throat and stood up. He started to speak, but his voice caught in his throat. He cleared it again as he got down on one knee.

"Janet, the time we spend together has been some of the happiest of my life. I love the way you laugh. I love how your brows draw together when you are concentrating. I love the way your face lights up when you see me walk in the room. Um, what I'm trying to say is I love you. Will you marry me?"

She only paused long enough to get down on his level, and placing her arms around his neck, she whispered 'yes'.

They were married in spring at the church with the whole congregation in attendance. The altar was decorated with green plants and pots of daffodils. Janet carried a bouquet of daffodils and white roses. A pastor friend from a neighboring church performed the ceremony and the kids from the church stood up with them. After all, it was thanks to them that the two had met. The ladies of the church had a huge spread of food for the meal after the vows. The kids tied tin cans to the back of Thomas's car and chased them halfway down the road when they left.

As they got to the little cottage, Thomas took Janet's hand in his and they walked together through the door. The church had placed vases of spring flowers all over and the whole cottage was transformed into a garden. Thomas brought Janet's hand up to his lips and placed a light kiss along the back of her knuckles. She smiled as she thought of how far her life had come since she had moved into her house. It now fairly glowed with happiness. The little cottage had truly become a home now, overflowing with happiness and the promise of a future.

Marlene & the Geek

The 1980s

Marlene was born into a simpler life. She grew up able to ride her bike around the neighborhood and didn't have to be home until the street lights came on. She walked to and from school until she got her first car. Her dad came home at five to eat the dinner her mom had spent all day preparing.

She had the same best friend since first grade, Jane, with whom she shared everything. They spent practically every waking moment at each other's house. If they weren't together, they were talking on the phone. They played dolls when they were little, then planned their perfect weddings when they grew older. Her early life was fun and innocent like an episode of her favorite show, The Brady Bunch.

High school was a blast for Marlene and Jane. They went to every football or basketball game and cheered their team to victory, though they were too shy to try out for cheerleader. Marlene became editor of the school newspaper with Jane as the top reporter.

They soon added two more to their group, Tammie and Michelle. They were as alike as peas in a pod, although Tammie was the more adventurous one. She was always coming up with a daring plan and saying they would laugh about it later. Michelle was the quiet, studious one. Yet everyone knew that you never would see one without the other three.

Nights were spent taking turns at each other's house for late night sleepovers, gossip, and the obligatory prank calls. If one of them got a boyfriend, they insisted that the other three went along on their dates. This was not a popular idea for most boys. So, their dating life was practically non-existent.

Not to say that they didn't have boyfriends. They hung around with a bunch of boys, more as a group. They were just 'boy' friends, not boyfriends. There was Lloyd the geek, Ricky and Gerald the twins because you never saw one without the other, and Frank the math nerd. They would volunteer as the girls' escorts if one was needed. They would go to parties as a group, no one showing favoritism over another. If anyone of them felt anything romantic, nothing was ever said.

Like all teenagers, Marlene didn't appreciate what she had when she had it. Her simple, idyllic way of life soon gave way to the changing 70's, an era of pushing boundaries. Music changed from The Monkees and The Partridge Family to Alice Cooper and Elton John. Clothing went from knee length skirts to super short minis. Hair on the boys went from neat crops to shoulder length, rivaling the girls long straight locks. Parties changed from hanging out listening to records to going off as couples and smoking.

Life had definitely changed and Marlene along with Tammie was on board with it. Their senior year in school was split between old friends and new party friends. The boys in their group became more focused on future plans like going to college. All they wanted to talk about was this new thing called a computer and how it was going to change the world. Marlene and Tammie found it incredibly boring and began to pull away from the little group. Marlene was sad she and Jane had grown apart, but Jane just wouldn't embrace this new lifestyle. Marlene had no choice but to leave her behind.

They managed to get together as a group a couple of times before graduation, but everyone could tell things had changed. They did get together to pose for a graduation picture at Lloyd's urging. He said it was for old time's sake. After his parents snapped the picture, everyone began to scatter to various parties.

Lloyd followed after Marlene, calling for her to wait up. He had not signed her yearbook yet.

"Oh, Lloyd. I'm in an awful hurry. Can't we do this another time?" She said as she continued to walk away.

"How about I take it with me and sign it? Then I can bring it by your house tomorrow."

In exasperation, she agreed and handed him the book.

"If I'm not home, just leave it with my parents. Okay?" and with that she was gone.

Lloyd spent the night pouring his heart out in a message for Marlene's yearbook. He wrote and rewrote, till his floor was littered with paper. He knew this was probably his last chance to let her see what she really meant to him. It was past midnight when he finally got it the way he wanted and transferred it over to the actual yearbook. He closed the book with a hope that Marlene would accept the love he had poured out for her.

The next morning, Lloyd drove over to Marlene's house. Mrs. Jeffries said Marlene was still asleep but she would be happy to give her the book when she woke up.

Lloyd waited expectantly for Marlene to call him. When days went by with no response, he had to admit his love was not returned. It was time to get on with his life. He had big plans and couldn't let this stop him. One dream may have ended, but luckily, he had others.

The next four years, her old friends went to college to get their degrees. Even Jane and Michelle went. They both went to school for business degrees with plans on being secretaries when they graduated. Marlene and Tammie got jobs at a department store.

They worked days and partied at night. Marlene rarely heard from the old gang. Their lives had gone completely different directions and seemed to know exactly what they wanted. Marlene and Tammie appeared content to go along with and embraced the decadent lifestyle of the 80s. They went to nightly parties where everyone just hung out, drinking, smoking, and listening to music.

Marlene lived at home with her parents since she couldn't afford a place on her own. Her mom and dad did not approve of her choices and complained all the time. They thought she was wasting her life. Marlene thought they were too old fashioned and controlling. She couldn't wait to move out on her own. She and Tammie decided to pool their money and find a small place together. They wouldn't have much money left for food, but as long as they had their smokes, they'd be okay.

Marlene saw a small notice on the bulletin board at the Piggly Wiggly advertising a cottage for rent. She pulled it off so no one else could get to it before she did. She placed a call to the owner as soon as she got back to work. She spoke with a Mr. O'Shaunessy who explained the amount of the rent, the due date, along with a lengthy description of the house. It all sounded fine, the only drawback-it was a one bedroom. Scared to lose such a deal, Marlene said they would take it. They agreed to meet that weekend to sign the papers and drop off the key.

Tammie was happy about their own place but not keen on having to sleep on the living room couch. Marlene won her over with descriptions of the fun parties they could have in their own house. She then changed the subject by mimicking Mr. O'Shaunessy and his strange little accent. They each took turns guessing what he would look like.

That weekend, they moved their clothes and everything else they owned from their parents' homes to the cottage. Mr. O'Shaunessy was there and tried to explain how to operate the gas stove and all the necessary upkeep the cottage would require of them. They paid little attention to anything he told them. He looked reluctant as he turned over the keys then left them with a warning that he would be checking in later.

At first, life in the little cottage was a blast for the two girls. They had just enough money to keep their smoking habit going and pay the rent. They made frequent trips to their parent's homes to stock their pantry with food. They only looked to the weekend ahead and the next party.

The fashions of the 80s were so fun and colorful. Marlene started asking for overtime so she could buy them; leg warmers, oversized shirts with bright colors, and high waisted jeans. A new singer, Madonna, was setting some of her own trends. Marlene loved to dress like her, pairing leggings, tulle skirt, and a large bow in her hair to go out to the clubs.

Tammie didn't believe in working overtime. Marlene often came home to find Tammie gone and her new clothes missing from her closet. They were returned, when she didn't have to hunt for them herself, torn and dirty. She was getting very tired of funding her friend's nights out.

She tried to talk to Tammie, but she just brushed Marlene off. Tammie had become the ultimate party girl and wouldn't listen to anything Marlene said. Sometimes Marlene wished she still had Jane and Michelle to talk to. She could definitely use their advice right now.

Marlene found out Tammie had planned a big party for that next Saturday. Tammie had taken care of everything on her own, thinking Marlene would be working. She had gone over to her parent's house and raided the pantry of any snacks. She told everybody it was BYOB, so all she had to supply was the mixers. It was going to be a blowout.

Tammie spread the word about the party and over seventy people showed up. Cars lined the little lane, flattening the azaleas that ran along it. People were spread out all over the cottage, practically bursting the little house at the seams. Music was blaring over huge speakers that someone had set up. The house was set so far back from the road that they didn't have to worry about neighbors complaining. The evening was warm enough to take the party outside. It was the perfect set up.

Marlene had been asked to work late that night and arrived home after ten o'clock to the party in full swing. She tried to find Tammie and ask her to call it an early night, but she was nowhere to be found. Marlene pushed her way into her bedroom only to find it full of people. She pushed and shoved them out. Then slammed the door and locked it. Sleep would be impossible, but at least she was alone.

The party lasted until the morning. When the sun was shining high through the windows, Marlene began to stir. As she walked into the living room, she was greeted with people sleeping

all over the furniture and floor. Trash littered every surface that wasn't covered with a body. She stepped gingerly over the 'guests' until she got to the kitchen. People were in there too. She managed to make herself a cup of coffee and took it out to the patio. There were people out there and even more trash.

Marlene was disgusted. She had grown to love the peace and quiet of the little garden on a Sunday morning. When had she allowed Tammie to take over the cottage? She felt she had no say any more about what went on here. Well, that was going to change. Her name was on the lease, not Tammie's, and if she didn't want to change then she would just have to pack up and leave. Marlene wasn't sure if she could swing everything on her own, but she had just gotten a raise at the store. If she cut out cigarettes and liquor, she should just be able to make it.

She picked up trash, not caring that she occasionally hit someone's foot or hand as she did so. By the time she was finished, she had managed to rouse all the people outside. She not so nicely told them to get out. She went into the kitchen and did the same thing. The living room was the worst. Tammie refused to get up and help. Marlene was steaming by the time she got everything cleaned up. It was time for a 'come to Jesus meeting' for her and Tammie.

Once everything was straightened up, Marlene made a pot of coffee and told Tammie to have a seat. She poured them each a cup, hoping it would sober Tammie up enough to talk.

"This cannot happen again, Tammie. I work late and come home to people and trash all over the place. What were you thinking inviting so many people? We'll be lucky if Mr. O'Shaunessy doesn't charge us extra for all the damage to the azaleas and the garden."

Tammie looked up with bloodshot eyes and replied, "Oh, get over yourself Marlene. You are really becoming a bore. The only thing that would have bothered you before about this was you had to work and miss it."

Marlene had to admit that was true or used to be. Lately, she was tired of staying out all night, waking up with a hangover, and smelling like stale cigarette smoke. Maybe she was finally growing up. Well it was about time.

"Tammie, I think it's time you move out."

"You've got to be kidding, Marlene. I pay my share of the rent, so you can't kick me out!"

"Tammie, my name is on the lease. So, if I say get out, you need to go. I'll pay back the portion you've paid for the remaining part of the month, but I need you to go now. Today."

"Oh, I'm out of here alright. Good luck paying the bills without my money, Marlene. You'll be begging me to come back."

Marlene turned and went into her bedroom. There was no sense arguing with Tammie. They clearly had different views of their respective futures.

When had her views changed? She had loved the party life. She had loved dressing up and going to clubs. She had loved the haziness that drinking afforded her. It had allowed her to forget everything for a little while.

She waited in her room until she heard Tammie's car turn down the driveway. The living room was a mess. Tammie had definitely taken out her anger on the furnishings. Marlene took her time straightening things. With each piece she set right, she thought of the different things in her life that she would like to set right again.

Marlene started out that afternoon with a visit to her parents. They were surprised to see her, it had been months. Their first thought was she needed money, that seemed to be all they were good for anymore. Then they noticed something seemed different about her. She was even dressed different. No more spiked hair, black jump boots, or short skirt. She was dressed in leggings, oversized men's shirt, and ballet flats. She looked so pretty. She even had a smile on her face, something they hadn't seen in a long time.

They were delighted to have her home. She even agreed to stay for dinner. It felt like a celebration, a return of the prodigal son. Marlene wondered why she had distanced herself from her parents. They didn't hold her past against her. They were still the loving, caring couple they had always been.

After dinner, Marlene went upstairs to her old bedroom. It was still the way it had been when she left. She plopped herself down on the bed and stared up at the ceiling. It felt good to be back. Not to live, no she was too used to her independence. But she made the decision to visit more often.

Marlene's hand fell down to the side of her bed. She felt something hard. It was a book, her yearbook. She had dropped it there after graduation and guessed mom had not noticed it, half covered by the bedspread. She ran her hand over the cover and memories came flashing back.

She hadn't bothered to read what anyone had written. Back then she hadn't cared. Now, suddenly, she did.

There were the usual one or two liners. 'Hope to see you this summer' and 'It was fun having class with you.' She quickly skimmed over those, looking for the ones that people had actually written something meaningful. Wow, a lot of people had cared enough to write some really nice things. She was pleasantly surprised and slightly humbled.

There was Tammie's. Lots of writing about how much partying they would be doing and hanging out together. Michelle's was very nice and talked about how much fun they had over the years. Jane's was bittersweet and made Marlene cry. She talked about all the things they had done since becoming friends in first grade. She talked about the times they had slept over at each other's houses and called boys up on the phone. She talked about all the plans they had talked about once they got out of school. The part about how much she missed spending time with her those last few weeks in school, made Marlene so sad and full of regrets. She felt bad for not staying in touch with Michelle and especially Jane. They had been as close as sisters at one time.

It was all her fault and she didn't know how to fix it. Could she just call up and apologize? Marlene didn't know. She felt she needed to get her life back on the right track before contacting anyone from her past. She wanted to able to go to them with her new outlook and them to see that she had changed.

There were the ones from Frank, Gerald, and Ricky, all reminiscing about the fun times they had shared. They wished her luck in the future and said they hoped to see her over the summer. Well, that had not happened. She and Tammie had started running with a new crowd and left them in the dust.

Marlene kept reading until she turned to the last page. There it was. She had been wondering what Lloyd had written. She vaguely remembered him asking for her yearbook at graduation. At first glance, she was surprised at the length of what he had written. She didn't remember him as being overly talkative.

Dear Marlene,

I hope you'll remember me. I know I'll always remember you and Jane. I thought you might like this:

What is love?

I only know that

I feel warmth

And happiness

When I am near you.

I feel complete trustfulness

And understanding

When I talk with you.

I feel a deep involvement

And interest

When I listen to you.

I feel as though I am

The sun, the moon, the trees

When we are together.

Is this love?

And isn't this better than love?

I hope you keep this poor expression of my feelings. I'll always keep the gifts and cards that you, Jane, Michelle, and Tammie gave me. I had better leave you alone before I bug you to death

Love always, Lloyd

B.K.A. The Geek

What? She fell back on her pillows, stunned. Love? Lloyd? Was he kidding her? Was it some kind of joke?

Marlene sat there for a few minutes, reading it again and again. She wasn't quite sure what to think about this. At first thought, she felt quite flattered and a small smile crossed her face.

Lloyd the Geek, in love with her. What a thing. It would take some time to digest this information.

She packed up her yearbook and a few other mementos to take back to the cottage. Hugging her parents goodbye, she promised to be back next week for another family dinner. The happy smiles on both their faces was all Marlene needed to know she was back on the right track.

Life alone in the little cottage was so peaceful without Tammie and her constant chaos. Marlene spent her days working at the department store and nights watching TV. Not as exciting as her former life, but it was starting to grow on her. The highlights of her week were watching Dallas and Knots Landing on Thursdays and surprisingly, having dinner with her parents. While things were still a little strained between them, it was slowly getting back to normal, or at least a new normal.

After finding her yearbook, Marlene could not stop thinking about her old friends and what they were up to now. She spent a lot of time thinking about Lloyd and wondered if he was still in town. She tried looking them up in the phone book, but couldn't find them. She found their parents, but was hesitant to reach out to them. She was worried what they must think of her and how she had acted. She decided contacting them would be her last resort.

One Saturday, her dad reached out and invited her to church. She hadn't attended in years and joked about being struck by lightning when she entered the building. Her dad did not find that funny and she felt silly for having said it. She agreed to go with them this one time as long as they didn't bug her to continue. She could feel their excitement over the phone.

Sunday morning, Marlene got up early, something she was not accustomed to doing on the weekends. She put on her most demure dress, a bright pink, knee length with small shoulder pads. Pink flats completed the outfit. Suddenly, she felt like a large flamingo. What had she been thinking when she bought this? Oh well, she didn't have time to change, so off she went.

Walking into the church was sobering. She was nervous. She had only been half joking with the lightning remark after all. She didn't feel like a lamb being welcomed back into the flock but more like a lamb being led to the slaughter. Taking a deep breath and straightening her padded shoulders, she went in with head held high. Yes, she had made mistakes, but isn't that what church was for. Forgiveness?

She walked down the aisle behind her parents, feeling like all eyes were on her. She knew it was ridiculous, it was just her guilt and shame making her feel that way. It felt like the preacher must have known she was coming, because it felt the sermon was directed right at her. She felt her cheeks blushing red.

Walking out of the church, she cringed every time her parents stopped to greet someone. She stood behind them with a smile plastered on her face, feeling like an imposter. She looked into the preacher's face as she shook his hand, but she didn't see any contempt, only a welcoming smile. Perhaps he hadn't intended that sermon to be so personal to her.

As they walked to the parking lot, an older couple came up to them. It was Michelle's parents. Why she hardly recognized them it had been so long. She was embarrassed to greet them because the way she had abandoned Michelle after graduation. But they did not hesitate. Michelle's mom reached out to envelope her in a big hug. Her dad reached his hand out for a hearty handshake. They both had a huge grin on their face as they greeted her and said how good it was to see her.

Marlene got up the nerve to ask how Michelle was doing. Her mom said she had moved to Knoxville after graduating college and was working as a legal secretary at a law firm there. She got married this last year to a nice lawyer and they had bought a house in Maryville. They were planning on starting a family within the next year and they couldn't be happier. She realized how she was going on about Michelle and her wonderful life and stopped awkwardly.

Marlene admitted to herself a sting of jealousy for Michelle's perfect life. But she was happy too that her friend had found happiness. She smiled at the proud mom and said how glad she was to hear how well Michelle was doing. On an impulse, she asked her mom to please tell her hi and that she had asked about her. She gave her another hug and said their goodbyes.

Her parents were quiet when they got in the car. She knew they thought she probably felt awkward at the meeting. But strangely she did not. It had been good to hear about Michelle. She actually felt happy for her friend and hoped her parents would give Michelle her message.

Well, with the question answered about one of her old friends, Marlene began to wonder how she could find the other ones, especially Lloyd. Why hadn't she thought to ask Michelle's parents some questions? She bet they knew where the rest of the old gang was and what they were doing. Maybe she'd ask next time, if she decided to go back to church.

With another raise at work, Marlene began to toy around with the idea of going to college. It would probably be expensive and take all her extra money, but what else did she have to spend it on? She was quite content in the little cottage, she didn't need a bunch of new clothes since she wasn't going out, and she ate a lot of nights at her parent's house. She took one of her lunch hours to go by the college and pick up the paperwork to apply. Luckily, her grades from high school had been decent, so no worries there.

She applied for financial aid and was accepted. Now, what major to choose? She thought back to her friends and how they had gone on and on about computers. They had been right and how she wished now she had followed their lead.

She decided to major in business administration and minor in computers. That way she could get a job in an office, even one at the department store where she worked now, if she wanted. A minor in computers could only help as they were showing up everywhere.

Life took on a predictable yet peaceful routine. She would go to work during the day, then take night classes over at the college. Church every Sunday became a weekly ritual and she looked forward to it and the meal afterward at her parent's house.

She had worked up the nerve to ask Michelle's parents about the other guys. They knew Jane was up in Boston, but they weren't sure what she was doing. Ricky and Gerald had graduated college and gone into business together. They weren't sure what it was exactly, but it had something to do with technology. Frank was working for an engineering firm in Nashville, but they couldn't remember the name of it. They didn't know what Lloyd was doing. They weren't a ton of help, but at least she knew her friends were all flourishing.

Months went by and she had not found out any more about her friends. Every so often, she got on the computer at school and tried to look them up. But no luck. One Sunday, to her delight, Michelle's parents told her Michelle was coming in that week for a visit. Marlene asked them to please see if she would like to meet up for lunch while she was in. She gave them her phone number and waited.

Michelle had accepted the invitation and she was meeting her that evening after work. Marlene was so nervous. What would she say? Should she apologize? Yes, probably. Wonder what Michelle looks like now? She was always so pretty. What would she think of her? Would she think she had changed? Hopefully.

Walking in, she blinked and looked around hoping to recognize her friend. She needn't have worried. As soon as she spotted her, Michelle stood up and came forward to hug her old friend.

"Marlene, you look wonderful. It is so good to see you. Sit down and let's catch up."

Marlene took in the slight bump under Michelle's top. "Congratulations Michelle! You look wonderful."

"Oh, I'm only at three months, but this baby is hungry all the time. Come on, let's order. We're both starving!"

Laughing, they each ordered and before the waitress could leave, they both began talking at once. It seemed just like yesterday they had last seen each other. They took up right where they had left off. It wasn't stilted at all. Marlene said a silent prayer of thanks. It felt so good to be back with her friend. They both talked about old times and laughed until they cried. Michelle never mentioned the fact she had turned her back on her friends and for that, Marlene was so grateful. She eventually got around to asking about the rest of the group.

Ricky and Gerald were out in San Francisco working hard at something called a start up internet company. They always said they would go into business together and it apparently was going well. Frank was at a top engineering firm in Nashville and was busy designing a new mall. She hadn't heard from Lloyd in a few months. The last she knew, he had taken a new job and was moving to Atlanta.

Marlene hesitated before bringing up Jane's name and Michelle seemed to sense her hesitation.

"Jane is living up in Boston now," Michelle said in answer to the silent question. "She's gone back to school to get her Master's degree to teach. She's actually dating a really great guy and they got engaged this past summer."

Marlene blinked back a tear. It hurt so much to hear how everyone's lives had gone on without her. She was sad at how much time she had wasted. But she was back now and with Michelle being so receptive to her, she could only hope and pray that the others would be too.

They finished the evening with a big hug, an exchange of phone numbers, and a promise to keep in touch.

Spring came to Tennessee with a burst of blooms. The little garden at the cottage came back to life after that disastrous party thanks to Marlene's careful attention. The azaleas along the lane were just beginning to bloom and splashes of pink and red greeted her every day. School was going well and she even made the dean's list this past semester. Life was certainly looking up and she couldn't be more grateful.

One afternoon, when Marlene stopped to get her mail, she saw a light pink envelope among the bills and advertisements. She pulled into the lane and couldn't go any further without seeing what it was. She thought it might be an invitation to a baby shower for Michelle, but to her surprise, it was a wedding invitation. It was an invitation to Jane's wedding. Oh, this was so unexpected, but oh how wonderful!

Marlene quickly sent in her RSVP and began planning the perfect outfit. It would be the first time she had seen anybody but Michelle since graduation and she wanted to look her best. This time she picked out a dusty rose dress with a dropped waistline. It had a large lace collar, pearl buttons down the front, and lightly padded shoulders. With her pearl colored hose and light beige shoes and purse, she felt she looked pretty good. She had recently gotten a perm, so her hair would look decent styled in tight curls.

The wedding day dawned bright and clear. Marlene was so nervous she could barely wait until time to leave. Michelle said all the old gang would be there. She had casually asked if Lloyd was coming, trying not to raise any suspicion about him in particular. She had been assured everyone said they would attend.

Her stomach was full of butterflies as she pulled up to the church. What if they didn't speak to her? What if she was ignored? No, she knew Michelle would be there for her even if the others were not. She shook her curls and walked up the steps and through the front door.

Standing at the front, serving as one of the ushers, was Frank. He looked up and gave her a wide smile. He stepped forward and enveloped her in a big hug.

"Marlene, it's so great to see you. Come on. I've got a seat for you with some of the old gang," he said as he stuck out his elbow for her to take.

Whew, well here goes. One down, four more to go.

When he stopped at one of the pews near the front, Marlene cautiously raised her eyes. There was Ricky and Gerald grinning at her. They beckoned for her to take a seat and began talking at the same time.

"Marlene, you look great kid. Come sit here between us so we can catch up before this thing gets started," Ricky said.

"You look fantastic, Marlene. It's so good to see you," Gerald broke in.

The people on the row in front of them, turned around and gave them all a look. Marlene couldn't help but laugh. It was so good to see them both. She gave them a quick hug and settled back into the pew.

After a few minutes, she couldn't help but ask about Lloyd.

"He's supposed to be here. He's only able to pop in for the ceremony and then leave. He's got some lecture scheduled in Nashville that he can't miss."

Marlene tried to hide her disappointment. Well, maybe she would get a chance to talk to him when he arrived. Surely, he would sit with them.

The music began and everyone turned to watch the bridesmaids start down the aisle. It looked like Lloyd wasn't going to make it after all. Just then, rushing in between Michelle, the matron of honor, and the bride, was Lloyd. He took a seat in the very back and Marlene watched as he gave Jane and her dad a small salute and smile as they walked by. She took in a few details before her attention was all on Jane.

Her former best friend was a vision. Her dress was row upon row of lace and satin. The sleeves were lace and gathered at her wrists with a line of satin covered buttons. The bodice was topped with an upright collar. Her veil reached halfway down the aisle and was covered with tiny seed pearls. She had never seen such a smile on her friend's face, she fairly glowed.

When the guests had been seated, Marlene snuck a quick glance back at Lloyd. Sadly, her vision was blocked by a large hat worn by the lady in front of him. She would just have to catch him after the ceremony. Surely, he would hang around to congratulate Jane and say hi to his friends.

The ceremony was beautiful. Jane spoke her vows in a whisper. Her groom's voice shook as he said his. Marlene wiped away tears as the couple said 'I do' and turned to the guests. It was like Jane looked right at her, smiling a big smile. Oh, she could only hope that she would be glad to see her.

It seemed like it took forever to make her way back down the aisle and to the reception being held downstairs. Ricky and Gerald kept up a running conversation as she tried to spot Lloyd in the crowd. They got in the reception line and Marlene held her breath as she got closer and closer to Jane. Suddenly, it was her turn to face her. Jane turned her head to greet her, the next guest, and her face broke into that same old grin that Marlene remembered. She reached out and grabbed Marlene and gave her the biggest hug. Tears shone in her eyes.

"Oh, Jane. You look so beautiful. Congratulations. Thank you for inviting me," Marlene managed to get out before being pushed down the line by the two guys. She shook the groom's hand, then hugged Michelle. She turned to go to their table, looking all the time for Lloyd's head above the crowd.

Later, Jane made her way to their table. Ricky got up and gave her his seat. Her veil was long gone but she still had that radiant smile on her face. Marlene felt a sudden shyness. What should she say after all this time?

Jane didn't wait for her to speak. She reached over and took Marlene's hand in her own. Her diamond engagement ring and accompanying wedding band glinted in the light. She paused a moment as if admiring the look of them, then laughed and squeezed Marlene's hand.

"Oh, Marlene. I can't tell you how happy I am you came. Remember how we would talk and dream about how we wanted our weddings to be? It just wouldn't have been the same without you here."

"Jane, I owe you the biggest apology. I am so, so very sorry for the way I acted."

"That's in the past Marlene. Let's leave it there. I'm just so happy that we were able to share this like we always dreamed of."

Marlene felt a sting of sadness as a thought that if things were different, she would have been Jane's maid of honor. But she shook that off and smiled.

"I see the boys found you. They have been so excited to see you again. That's all they could talk about. It's a shame Lloyd had to rush off to that lecture. I'm sure he would have loved to have seen you too."

Her heart sunk. Lloyd had already left without getting a chance to say a word to him? When would another opportunity come along? Would she have to wait for someone else to get married? She could only hope that opportunity would come before too long.

"Oh, what a shame," Marlene managed to say. "How is Lloyd? Is he seeing anyone? Has he gotten married yet?"

Jane smiled at the questions. "No, as far as I know he's not seeing anyone special. Funny you should ask. I always got the impression that he kind of liked you back in school. He always managed to sit beside you in class or in the car. Looking back now, it seemed pretty obvious."

Marlene blushed and changed the subject. "I want to hear everything. Where are you going on your honeymoon? Where are you going to live?"

"We're going to Gatlinburg for our honeymoon. The mountains should be beautiful with all the flowers blooming now. Then we head back to Boston. Look, let's exchange phone numbers and once we get back and settled, I'll give you a call and we can catch up on everything. Maybe sometime you can come up to Boston and I can show you around." Jane was interrupted by her new husband coming up.

"Darling, I have some relatives I want you to meet," he said and smiled an apology to Marlene.

Jane leaned over and gave Marlene a kiss on the cheek. "I'm so glad to see you and I'll give you a call soon." And with that she was gone.

Marlene spent some time catching up with Ricky and Gerald. Frank and Michelle joined them and they talked as if they had been together just yesterday. It was wonderful and Marlene could not think of a time she had enjoyed more. Her only regret was not getting to talk to Lloyd.

Time went on and Marlene kept busy with work and school. She had been invited to Michelle's baby shower. The three girls spent the weekend together with most of the time spent talking over old times. The baby was born a month later, a girl, Elizabeth Jane, and the girls came together to welcome her home. Marlene casually asked about Lloyd again.

"The boys tell me he's busy going all over the country working and giving lectures on some new technology. They haven't been able to pin him down either. I do get a letter from him occasionally," Jane said. "Oh, and can you believe it? He's still not seeing anyone seriously. I guess he's just too busy to settle down."

Marlene couldn't help but smile to herself. She had really built that writing in her yearbook into something. She knew so much time had passed that there might not be anything there anymore. But still she hoped.

Fall semester started and Marlene worked her schedule so she could take classes during the day and work at night. This way she could get her degree faster. It turned out she liked the computer classes so much that she was decided to double major.

She was also teaching Sunday school at church and loving it. She still attended regular church with her parents, but now they switched up cooking Sunday dinner. Her parents loved the coziness of the little cottage and except for it being so far back alone in the woods, they felt she was safe there. She could barely remember how her life had been before. God had truly worked a miracle in her.

One day, she saw a notice of an upcoming lecture on computers and their future use in home and business. It sounded very interesting and her teachers highly recommended they all attend.

Later that week, she walked in, taking a seat in the back. She dragged out her pen, notebook, and mini tape recorder to get ready. A man came in, stepped up to the lectern, announced the lecture title, and introduced himself. She almost fell out of her chair when she heard his name, Lloyd Austin.

What? After all this time, he just walks into her lecture hall? What were the odds?

Marlene tried not to make it noticeable as she looked over every inch of him. He was tall with wavy brown hair that still had a cowlick in the back that would not be tamed. Suddenly she wanted to put her hands in his hair, run her hands through it, and pat that cowlick into place. Get a hold of yourself woman, she admonished herself.

She tried to concentrate on what he was saying. She even attempted to take notes, but she couldn't think of anything except there he was, standing right in front of her. She watched as his eyes wandered around the room as he spoke. She saw the puzzled look in his eyes when he first glimpsed her. He looked surprised and a small smile crossed his face before he turned his attention to the other rows of students.

Did he end the lecture quicker after he saw her? She wasn't sure, but she liked to think so. She waited impatiently as the other students shook his hand and asked a few follow up questions. Finally, it was her turn to step up. Her hand trembled a little as she stuck it out to shake his.

"Hi, Lloyd," was all she could manage to get out.

"Hello, Marlene," was all he could say.

They both broke out into a big smile and laughed.

"You'd think we could think of more to say to each other after all these years, wouldn't you?" she asked.

"Oh, yes. I should think so. How about I buy you a cup of coffee after I finish up here and we catch up?"

Marlene couldn't say yes fast enough.

Amy
and
Christopher
The 1990s

Amy and Christopher met their senior year in high school. They went to rival schools and happened to meet at a football game in line for the snack bar.

Amy noticed the tall boy in line and maneuvered her way behind him. She even managed to 'accidentally' bump his arm.

"Oh, I'm so sorry. I didn't mean to bump you."

He turned around, ready to say something about being more careful. But stopped once he saw her.

"Oh, that's okay. I should be the one apologizing. I probably stepped back into you," he said with a smile.

He continued the conversation with some mild teasing about their team going to win the match up and she responded back with a smile and a declaration of 'no way'. They kept up the friendly banter until they had been served their food. They both stood there awkwardly until not wanting the connection to end, Christopher took her drink in his other hand. He nodded for her to go first and followed her back to her seat.

He endured some good-natured teasing as he sat down beside her. His baseball cap and t-shirt bearing his school's name and mascot was glaringly obvious but he didn't care. He was so captivated by the girl's big brown eyes that any other thought went right out of his head. He spent the rest of the second half beside her asking questions. At the end of the game, he was a goner. They exchanged phone numbers and promised to call the next day.

That was how their love story started. He claimed he was the one that noticed her first, and she let him believe it.

Christopher called that night, to make sure she got home alright. They talked till two in the morning, making plans to meet the next day after they both got off work. Christopher worked weekends at the movie theatre and Amy worked afternoons and weekends in the mall food court. Both jobs didn't finish that night until well after ten, but they didn't care.

He spent all Saturday morning washing and waxing his truck to make sure it was good and shiny for his date that night. He was very proud of his truck. It was a lowered Chevy S-10 with tinted windows, chrome tailpipe, and custom paint job. He had spent most of his paycheck getting it just the way he liked it. He really wanted to impress Amy. She told him how much she liked his truck and he beamed with pride.

He was very polite, opening and closing the door for her. They ran through the drive-thru and got two drinks and an order of fries. She told him she wasn't hungry, but wound up eating most of his food anyway.

They talked a little about school and what kind of grades they made. He was a steady B/C and she was a straight A student. At first, that intimidated him, but she didn't use big words and act like she was smart, so soon he forgot about it.

Of course, since they were seniors, they had to ask about college. He was going to go to a trade school for auto repair. He loved tinkering around on his and his friends' cars. She had plans to go to a four-year college and major in graphic art.

They talked so long that her voice grew hoarse. He stopped and got her another drink. He took her back to the mall to pick up her car, waiting while she got it started and headed out of the parking lot.

"Call me to let me know you got home, okay?"

She smiled. "Of course."

That phone call lasted another three hours and the sun was coming up when they finally said goodbye.

Amy and Christopher dated all that year. They went to both schools' homecoming and at the end of the year, both proms. Christopher stayed to see Amy to walk for graduation and then ran to his own across town. They had a joint party at Amy's house with all their friends dropping by after their own family parties ended.

Their summer was spent working but every spare moment they were together. Neither one could imagine life without the other one.

Before Amy finished college, Christopher graduated trade school and had a good job at the local dealership. He earned a good wage and had nice regular hours, allowing him time to spend lots of time with Amy. He had saved all his spare money the past three years. No more spending it on his truck. He had big plans for his money now. It was time to ask Amy to marry him and he was ready to start their future life together.

He waited until one night when Amy was studying at the library and drove over to her parents' house. He sat nervously on the edge of the sofa and his voice shook as he asked them for Amy's hand in marriage. He knew it was kind of old fashioned, but having their blessing was very important to him and he wanted to start their marriage off on the right foot.

When Amy walked for her graduation, no one cheered louder than him. They had a small party at her parents' house afterward and Amy wondered why Christopher was acting strange and unusually quiet. As the sun turned into an orange ball in the sky, he took her hand and told everyone goodbye. They drove around town for a little while before going to a local park where they had spent many hours walking the trails. He asked her to close her eyes and wait in the truck a minute. She heard him rustling around in the back of the seat and almost peeked. His car door shut and she heard him walking around.

Soon he came back, opened her door, and took her by the hand. Making sure she kept her eyes shut, he led her around to a spot in front of the truck. Still holding her hand, he told her to open her eyes. Spread on the ground was the quilt her grandma had made for her when she was a little girl. On the quilt were red rose petals. Before she could say anything, he let go of her hand and dropped to one knee.

"Amy, you know that I love you more than life itself. I will do everything in my power to love and protect you for the rest of our lives. Please say you will marry me."

And he brought a blue box out from behind his back with a sparkling diamond ring nestled inside.

She bent down and wrapped her arms around his neck and exclaimed with an excited yes!

He carefully placed the ring on her finger and kissed the palm of her hand. Standing, he helped her up and kissed her again. This time the kiss lingered. Then he stood her back from him and told her he had one more surprise. Just then their families stepped out from the woods along the path, all cheering. They rushed up to the couple, hugging them, and asking to see the ring. One of her friends was there with a camera to catch the celebration. It was so special, that Amy began to cry at the sheer joy of it all.

They were married that fall in an outdoor wedding. The weather was beautiful and the brightly colored leaves were a stunning backdrop for the sunflowers used in the bouquets. The guests were seated on bales of hay covered with colorful quilts. Amy wore a white gown, with an overlay of embroidery. Her hair was in a simple braid down her back. Everyone agreed that they had never witnessed such a beautiful, sincere exchange of vows. The couple's faces fairly shone with their love for each other. It was a beautiful start to their life together.

With some help from their parents, they were able to save up and buy a little house in a new subdivision near their jobs. They went to flea markets and antique shops on the weekends and bought unique things to furnish their home. Half the fun was being together. Finding a treasure was icing on the cake. Christopher loved to grill and their parents were frequent guests at impromptu weekend gatherings. They joined a couple's class at church and hosted many get togethers.

Life was just what they had dreamed. The only thing they didn't have, were children. They were both an only child and talked often of having a house full of kids. They began to save their money in preparation of the upcoming expenses. But things have a funny way of happening when you least expect it.

Amy's alarm went off for the second time that morning. She was just so tired. The thought of going to work seemed too much for her today. She forced herself to sit up but quickly laid back down. The room was spinning and she felt sick to her stomach. The flu had been going around and of course, she had put off getting her shot. It would serve her right if she had it now, after fussing at Christopher to go ahead and get one. Well, at least, hopefully he wouldn't get sick if that's what she had.

She called out from work and managed to get to the kitchen and make a cup of tea. That helped, but she still felt queasy. She called into her doctor's office and wonder of wonders, they had a cancellation and could get her in. She got dressed and only ran to the bathroom once. It was definitely the flu. That was the only time she ever threw up.

The doctor agreed that the flu was going around and gave her both a strep and flu test. The strep was negative and the doctor paused and turned to study her intently for just a second.

"Hmm, Amy, do you think you could be pregnant? The nausea and exhaustion could be either one. How about we do a pregnancy test and just rule that out?"

Amy agreed and while they took the blood necessary for the test, she thought back to the last month. Yes, it was a possibility. She had been so busy at work lately, she had forgotten to keep up with the dates. But now was not the right time. They had not saved up all the money they had wanted. What would Christopher think? Would he be upset?

Knowing the results would take a few days, Amy decided not to say anything to Christopher. Why worry him for nothing? She stopped and bought a cola hoping to settle her stomach. It helped a little, but now her nerves were joining in the fun. She felt she would go crazy waiting for the results. Once home, she took a nap until Christopher came in. He was so sweet, taking care of her and fixing dinner. She woke up the next morning feeling a little better and managed to go back to work. One day down, one more to go.

She got the call at work. Yes, she was definitely pregnant. Her hand shook as she hung up the phone. What would Christopher say? Well, she would find out tonight.

Amy got home before he did and fixed his favorite dinner. It took all she had not to rush back and forth to the bathroom, but she managed to get it done. He came in and was surprised to see dinner already prepared. Their custom was usually to fix the meal together. He held her chair out and sat down across from her.

"Not that I'm complaining, but what's the special occasion? My favorite meal ready when I walk in the door and candles on the table. Did I miss an anniversary or something?"

Amy was nervous, but as she raised her eyes to his and smiled, he caught on.

"No. Are we really? Are you sure? When did you find out? Is it a boy or a girl? Oh, that's right, we won't know yet, will we? I don't care, as long as he's healthy. When will he get here? Oops, I said he, didn't I? Girl or boy, I really don't care." And he jumped up from his chair, ran around the table and scooped her up in his arms.

Amy's voice shook as she asked him, "I know we hadn't planned for it to happen so soon. We wanted to save up more money. But it just happened, you know?"

Christopher held her back at arm's length. She saw the big grin on his face, the loving glow in his eyes and knew everything would be alright. He drew her back into his arms. She heard him whisper into her hair, "I couldn't love you more than I do at this moment."

They wanted to wait a few months before telling their parents but they knew instantly by the goofy grins on their faces what was happening. They were thrilled. Plans were made for baby showers and decorations for the nursery. It was all too much for the men, so they adjourned to the den and turned on the game.

It seemed like baby plans had taken over their lives. They still cooked dinner together, but he insisted on doing the dishes. They each cleaned the house, but he always ran the vacuum and mopped. While they loved every minute of planning, they also wanted to enjoy the remaining time they had to be just a couple. They would go to movies on the weekends and picnics in the park, followed by short hikes along the trails. At least once a week, they went out to eat. There was something so sweet, how Christopher would place his hand on the small of Amy's back when they walked. He would help her in and out of the car. He was so protective and she loved the extra attention.

One night, Christopher surprised her with tickets to a play in Nashville. It was the one she had been waiting to see and was glad it was here before the baby came. They took the occasion to get all dressed up and he planned for dinner at a downtown restaurant before the play started. After their meal, they decided to walk the three short blocks to the theatre. They were so involved in their conversation, they didn't notice someone following them. It wasn't until they stepped out from under the street light that he made his move.

He stepped up quietly behind Amy and stuck something in her back. Christopher turned at once when Amy stopped walking. His brain registered the look of fear on her face. Then he saw the man behind her with what looked like a gun in his coat pocket shoved in Amy's back.

"Give me your wallet and nobody will get hurt," the man snarled.

When Christopher hesitated, the man shoved the gun farther into Amy's back.

"Now you don't want me to shoot her, do ya? Now give me that wallet!"

Christopher's brain was going a million miles a second. He had to protect Amy and the baby at all costs. How did he know that once he handed over his wallet, that the man might not still shoot them? He had an idea.

Christopher reached in his back pocket for his wallet. When he removed it, he pretended to fumble and drop it on the sidewalk.

It was only a split second, but the man glanced down at the wallet and his hand at Amy's back moved away. Christopher took that opportunity and punched the man in the jaw. He didn't want to take a chance on him getting back up and shooting them. The man fell back, landing on the sidewalk, and hitting his head on the concrete parking bumper in the adjacent parking spot. Christopher grabbed Amy's hand, practically running to the closest restaurant. He asked for the manager and told him to call the police. He seated Amy at a table and waited for them to arrive.

When the officers arrived, Christopher explained what had happened and walked with them to where he had left the man. To his surprise, the man was still lying there. Why hadn't he run away? Had he knocked him out? Apparently. The first officer leaned down and checked the man. He stood back up and shook his head. The other officer took Christopher by the arm and led him to the patrol car. He motioned for him to sit in the back seat and proceeded to take his statement. Within a minute, he could hear more sirens and an ambulance pulled up.

After checking the man, they covered him with a sheet and loaded him into the ambulance. A detective arrived along with another officer who took pictures of the scene. The detective came over and asked Christopher to go over his statement again for him. Christopher repeated what had happened, then asked if he could go check on his wife. An officer went with him to the restaurant and he was able to see Amy. The officer took down her statement. Amy turned to Christopher with a look of horror on her face when he told her what had happened to the robber.

"We're going to have to take you in to the station, sir. We will need to get your official statement and there will be some questions the detective will want to ask you."

"What about my wife?"

"She will need to answer some questions also. Do you have your car nearby?" At Christopher's nod, the officer said, "Then she can follow us to the station." With that he rose and took Christopher back out to the patrol car.

The rest of the evening was a nightmare. They put them in separate rooms and questioned them for several hours. They finally let Amy go, but based on the evidence, they would be booking Christopher on manslaughter charges. When they both protested, he said they could tell it all to the judge when Christopher appeared for arraignment. Right now, he would be booked and bail would probably be set.

Amy called both sets of parents while Christopher was taken off. While he was fingerprinted and photographed, Amy sat and waited for their arrival. She tried to explain what had happened, and they were as shocked as she was. He had been defending them from being robbed and possibly shot. Why on earth were they arresting him?

They tried to get Amy to go home and lie down. But she was determined not to leave until she could leave with Christopher. No amount of arguing would change her mind.

During Christopher's initial appearance, they learned that no weapon had been found on the man or anywhere near him. The judge took this into consideration when he set bail. Christopher's dad went straight to a bail bondsman and got everything settled for him to be released that night. After a ten-hour ordeal, Christopher was finally released and Amy's mom and dad drove the couple home. His parents followed in the couple's car. The first thing they did when they arrived was make Amy sit down with a cup of tea, a sandwich, and prop her feet up. She didn't want any fuss made over her, but she could tell it made Christopher feel better to be taking care of her, so she allowed it.

It was late that next day when the parents left them alone to rest. Christopher's dad had called an attorney friend of his and set up an appointment for the following day. He advised that they get on this as soon as possible.

The next morning, Amy could tell Christopher had been up for hours. He had her a healthy breakfast already waiting on a plate at the table. He sat down across from her, and even though she protested she had no appetite, he insisted she eat for the baby. She ate as much as she could, offering him bites off her plate. He ate a little to appease her. They both showered and dressed for the visit with the lawyer.

The lawyer was an older man with graying hair and a kind face. He could see the stunned expressions on the couple's faces as they entered his office. Their hands remained clasped tightly together as they sat on the leather sofa. He nodded as he had them both give their account of the incident. He made lots of notes, interrupting them for clarifications along the way. When they finished, he hesitated before he spoke.

"I have a copy of the police report and they are claiming you used unnecessary force that resulted in an unarmed man's death. I know you thought he was armed and feared for your lives. That is what we intend to show. It is not going to be easy. They have a newly elected prosecutor that is anxious to prove himself."

"What should we do for now? I've never had so much as a parking ticket before. I've never even been inside a courtroom until the other night."

"Right now, just leave everything to me. You take your wife home and you both get some rest. Go to work Monday and do not talk about the case on the advice of your lawyer. Usually that shuts most people up."

Christopher and Amy shook his hand then immediately took hold of each other's. They walked out of the lawyer's office still in a state of shock but hopeful that the man would take care of what was a big misunderstanding.

The couple tried to carry on with their lives as best they could. They felt their life alternated between living under a microscope or being ignored. People did not know what if anything to say to them, but they heard whispering behind their back everywhere they went. They met with their lawyer every week, but he just kept telling them not to worry. How do you not worry? That's what he should be telling them.

Amy's pregnancy was going along easier than expected. The doctor did several ultrasounds due to the extreme pressure she was under. But thankfully, everything was progressing just as it should. She did have to be put on occasional bed rest when her blood pressure went too high. Christopher could always calm her down and get it back under control.

The arraignment was scheduled fairly quickly. The new prosecutor was anxious to get his first win under his belt. Christopher pled not guilty and the trial was set two months out. His lawyer protested the need for such a speedy trial, but was overruled. The meetings with his lawyer increased to twice weekly. He wanted to make sure both Christopher and Amy's stories were exactly the same. He didn't want any surprises during the trial. He was still cautiously optimistic that the outcome would be favorable.

The trial began on a rainy overcast Wednesday morning. Amy promised Christopher that if she attended, she would remain calm. He made her parents promise to keep a close watch on her and take her out if need be. At seven months, he didn't want to risk her going into labor prematurely.

The prosecutor began with his opening statement. He declared Christopher used excessive force on an unarmed man, causing him to die at the scene. He went on for almost twenty minutes just with his statement. It sounded more like a campaign speech to all in the courtroom. Finally, it was time for Christopher's lawyer to speak. You could tell it had been awhile since he had tried a case in open court. He was semi-retired and had agreed to take this case as a personal favor to Christopher's dad. Now Amy was questioning if they had made the right decision.

There were not a lot of witnesses to call. There were the responding officers who confirmed no type of weapon was found at the scene. Which Christopher's lawyer had to agree with. There were some people who knew the victim and testified that he was as gentle as a lamb and had never threatened anyone. Christopher's lawyer cross examined each one. But could not get them to admit to any previous violence.

That was another thing that bothered Amy. Weren't they supposed to be the victims in this instance? Weren't they the ones that were held up? Why was the robber being betrayed as the victim? They had not gone out looking for him, had they?

Soon it was Amy's time to take the stand. She was a sympathetic sight as she wobbled up to take the oath. Tears were shining in her eyes as she told the story of the holdup. She testified that she had believed it was a gun pressed up against her back and that she feared they all might die. The prosecutor tried to trip her up, but she stood her ground.

Christopher had been advised not to take the stand, but it went against his better judgement not to speak up for himself. There were some character witnesses for him, but the prosecutor made them look like they were repeating what they had been told to say.

Too soon, the judge sent the case to the jury. They were only out three hours. Christopher stood up at the defense counsel table, his back ramrod straight. Amy, sitting behind him, could see how hard his body was shaking. She wanted to reach out and take his hand, to let him know she was there for him, but she had been told not to. She finally had to sit on her hands to keep from reaching out.

The jury foreman passed the verdict to the judge, who read it, then passed it back. None of the jurors made eye contact with Christopher and he knew from watching Law & Order, that was not a good sign. But he still had faith. He closed his eyes and said a quick prayer. He could feel Amy's eyes on him and he prayed that no matter the verdict, she would have the strength to get through this. That they would be granted the chance to raise their child together.

The foreman cleared his throat. Guilty. There was silence at first, then outraged voices broke out across the courtroom. Christopher turned around as Amy stood up and they grabbed hold of each other. Amy began to cry uncontrollably. He tried to calm her, but the bailiff came to take him back to await sentencing. The prosecutor announced that they would proceed due to his time restraints for the future.

After a short wait, Christopher was brought back in. He reached over to take Amy's hand and she felt how his hand trembled. She gave him a small smile and squeezed his hand. She mouthed 'I love you' before the judge returned and the sentencing began.

The judge heard arguments from both sides regarding sentencing. He paused a minute, then announced Christopher would be required to serve fifteen months in prison for the charges. The courtroom once again gasped. Christopher was led away to begin his sentence. He did manage to tell Amy he loved her.

After he left, the families gathered around Amy. They insisted she sit down and put her feet up on the seat. Her mom began fanning her. Her dad stood guard over her as other people began to push closer to get her reaction. They got her out of the courtroom as quickly as they could and took her back to her parent's home.

They insisted Amy rest, but she couldn't. Her mind was already planning. Christopher had not done anything wrong. He had just been protecting her and the baby. The whole thing was a terrible accident. There must be something they could do. Wasn't there an appeal process or something? She fell into a fitful sleep, thinking of what Christopher must be going through.

Both sets of parents had been planning too. They did not want Amy alone in her house as close as she was to delivering. They agreed that Amy should move back in with her parents. She could even stay after the baby was born. They would all pitch in and help out. Now they just had to get Amy to see the rationality of their plan.

At first, Amy did not want to consider leaving her home. She wanted to cocoon herself there and wait for Christopher to come back. She could not believe this was actually happening to them. It had just been an innocent night out and it had turned into a nightmare.

After a few nights alone in their house, she had to face the reality that Christopher was not coming home right away. Common sense told her she would need help with the baby and since her parents were willing, she decided to move back home for the time Christopher would be away.

As soon as Christopher had been processed and the required thirty day waiting period expired, Amy arranged to go visit him at the prison. She submitted the necessary papers the first week and been approved. She paid special attention to her dress and makeup. She didn't want him worrying about her and the baby.

Entering the prison was surreal, like something from a movie. She went through the required checkpoints and metal detector. Finally, she and Christopher were face to face. His eyes looked worried as he took in every detail.

He started talking first. "How are you? How is the baby? When was your last doctor visit and what did he say? How are the folks doing? Are they keeping an eye on you?" His questions came out in a rush.

She smiled softly at him. "I'm fine. The baby's fine, growing every day. The doctor said a few more weeks to go, but everything is going according to schedule. The folks are taking good care of me. In fact, they insisted I stay with them right now. They want to keep a close eye on me."

Christopher visibly relaxed a little. "That's good, sweetie. I'm glad you're staying with them. I'd worry about you being home alone right now."

They sat a few minutes in silence, just looking into each other's eyes. They didn't have to say a word. The love they shared was palpable. It could be felt in the small distance between them.

Amy broke the silence to tell him her idea. She was so excited she had to share it. "I think we should appeal your sentence. I've been reading up on stuff and I think we might have a case. What do you think?"

"I don't know Amy. Won't that cost a lot of money? With me in here and you out on maternity leave, maybe we should just leave it alone?"

"But honey, there were so many things that weren't right about your trial. We should fight to get your name cleared and get you out of here."

"You don't need to be worrying about this right now. You need to concentrate on the baby."

"I am thinking of the baby. We want you with us right now and I'm willing to do anything I have to do."

"Amy, I appreciate it, but I can make it and once I serve my time, we will be together. I don't want you to make any rash decisions. Please say you'll run everything by our parents before you rush into anything."

"I will, I promise." And with that, she dropped the subject and they spent the rest of their time talking about the baby.

Amy visited Christopher whenever allowed. She had taken a leave from her job for the trial and was off now until her maternity leave was over. They had already moved the nursery over to her mom and dad's and she was left nothing to do but wait and think.

She contacted several lawyers and explained the situation. Most were unwilling to take the appeal case. They didn't want to make enemies of the prosecutor. Finally, she found one, a young lawyer, eager to make a name for himself. He agreed that Christopher's trial had a lot of questionable things to it. She gave him details over the phone and he agreed to look into it. He explained the cost and Amy cringed. But really, what was the cost of Christopher's freedom worth?

The baby, a boy, was born early in the morning two months to the day that Christopher had gone to prison. As soon as they were both able, Amy arranged a visit. She dressed the baby up in a cute onesie for his first time to see his daddy. She put on makeup and the only dress that she could fit into right now and the two headed out. Her parents weren't thrilled about taking a young baby to the prison, but Amy insisted. Christopher needed to see his son. She hoped it would cheer him up as his voice grew more disheartened with each phone call. She was afraid he had given up and that would not do.

Christopher's eyes lit up as Amy walked into the room with the tiny bundle in her arms. One look at that little face and his eyes filled with tears. Life was so unfair. He should have been the one driving Amy to the hospital. The one holding her hand during labor. The first one to hold his son. He should be home with her now, instead of her bringing his son to see him in prison. He looked up at Amy and said how sorry he was, that he could never make it up to her, but he'd spend the rest of his life trying.

It broke Amy's heart to see Christopher so crushed in spirit. She hoped seeing his son would cheer him up, but despite his joy at the baby, he looked heartbroken. Should she tell him of her decision to go ahead and hire that lawyer? No, she didn't want to hear his arguments. Besides, she had already mailed him the last of their savings for a retainer.

When Amy felt better, she set up an appointment with the appeal lawyer. He told her his strategy and how much he proposed the cost would be. It was a larger sum than she had realized, but she told him to proceed. She would figure out how to get the money, she had to.

Amy came up with a plan. She and the baby were already living with her parents. Her and Christopher's house was just sitting empty. What if she sold their house? They should have just enough equity built up to pay the lawyer. She ran the plan by both sets of parents. Of course, they protested. They offered to put a second mortgage on their own homes, but Amy would not allow it. They had already spent all their savings on the first trial and she knew Christopher would not be happy to put their future in jeopardy again.

That next day, Amy called a realtor and put the house on the market. She didn't tell Christopher. She had his power of attorney while he was in jail, so she was able to sign all the paperwork. The house was in such a desirable part of town, that there were several offers within a week of it being on the market. Amy took the highest bid and arranged for their furniture to be moved to the parents' garages.

Soon, she was able to give the lawyer his money. Now, she just had to explain herself to Christopher. She prayed that he would see the wisdom in this and not be too angry. The lawyer wanted to see him as soon as possible, so she couldn't put it off any longer. She dressed up in Christopher's favorite dress and fixed her hair the way he liked it. She didn't believe that would make a difference, but it couldn't hurt either.

Christopher was happy to see her, but looked surprised to see her without the baby. A close look at her solemn face and his heart skipped a beat. "Is the baby alright? Are you alright? Is it the folks? Are they okay? I can tell by your face that something is terribly wrong. Please just tell me."

Amy was so focused on what she was going to say, that she hadn't thought to where his mind might go. "No, honey, everybody is fine. The baby is growing like a weed. Here see. I brought you a picture of him with your folks. I just needed to talk to you about something and I needed your full attention."

He breathed a sigh of relief and smiled a sad smile as he looked at the picture. Oh, how he wished he could be there with them right now. When he looked back up at Amy, her anxious look made him hastily put the picture down. "What's going on, Amy? Out with it. I'm not in the mood for a guessing game right now."

She bit her lip and decided to just come out with it. "Okay. Well, I've found a lawyer to take your appeal case. He looked at all the notes from the trial and thinks things went on that just weren't right. He feels like we have a good case for an appeal that will get you out of here and possibly get this whole thing wiped from your record."

Christopher didn't know what to say. He had resigned himself to being here until his sentence was served. He had given up all hope of getting out any sooner, let alone filing an appeal. For a second, his hope rose. Then he came back to reality.

"Amy, we don't have any money left. How would we even begin to pay him? We can't ask our parents to give us any more money, I just won't do it. It was a great idea and I appreciate you going to all that trouble, but we just can't do it."

"But we can, Christopher. Now just let me say what I want to say without you interrupting me. I've done a lot of thinking on this. The most important thing in the world is you, me, and the baby being together. That is all that matters to me. Clearing your name would be a bonus. But getting you out of here and back with us is the main thing."

"What's going on Amy? What have you done?"

"Well, don't get mad. Promise? I had to do it and I'm praying you'll understand."

"Out with it Amy."

"I sold the house. There I said it. Now I can see you're getting upset but let me explain. I wasn't living in the house. It was just sitting there empty, costing us money. My parents are fine with us staying with them for a while. So, I sold it. I got a great price for it. More than enough to pay the lawyer," she said in a rush. "When we get all this settled, we'll get another house. One with only happy memories in it. The folks are storing our furniture until we need it, so that's not costing us anything. I'm sure once you think about it, you'll agree that it was the only thing to do." She shot him a weak smile. She had felt much braver when she had practiced this speech at home.

Christopher felt like his head was going to explode off his shoulders. What had she done? Selling our house, our home, was she crazy? He wanted to yell. He wanted to tell her how foolish she had been, but looking into her frightened yet hopeful face, stopped him. He had no idea what all she had been dealing with. He was stuck inside these walls and couldn't imagine everything she had taken care of. He took a deep breath and asked God to guide his words.

"Honey, I really wish you had asked me first before you did anything so permanent. I was willing to wait out my sentence. No, I don't like it, but I didn't want to put our future at more risk than it already is. Why didn't you talk to me? We should have discussed this together."

"I knew you would tell me not to. I knew you would put me and the baby first and I wanted to put you first for a change. You don't deserve to be here. You should be home with us, we need you. This is our only chance to get you back home now. Please know that I didn't do this without a lot of thought and prayer. It was only a house I sold. There is no home without you there and it never could be. We will figure out everything else once we get you out of here."

He let out a long sigh. What good would it do to berate her over her decision now? What could he do anyway? What's done is done. He took a deep breath in, changed the expression on his face and decided to accept what it was.

"Okay. Now tell me everything the lawyer said. If I'm going to get out of here, I want to start right away."

Amy drew in a shaky breath, relieved that his anger had subsided. She began to fill him in on what the lawyer wanted to do.

The appeal case was going well. The lawyer met with Christopher and Amy every week. Their money was holding out, so Amy took a permanent leave from her job to concentrate on the baby and the case. After a few weeks, the lawyer told her to expect Christopher home within the next two months. They were just awaiting a court date and he was very confident that he could get both the sentence and the charges dropped.

Amy began to plan. She wanted to give them a fresh start. She knew they could remain living with her parents, but after so much time apart, she wanted it to be just the three of them. She started looking for an apartment to rent. To her delight, she saw an ad for a cottage in a small town next to theirs. She placed a call to the owner right away.

Mr. O'Shaunessy, the owner, told her another person had already called about the cottage. However, after listening to Amy's story, he agreed to give her first chance at it. She met the little man that afternoon and was delighted at her first glance at the cottage. Its red brick glowed with a warmth from the sun and the large windows beckoned her to come take a look. After touring the little house, she knew it was the perfect place for them to heal from their past and start over again. Even though it only had one bedroom, it had room for a crib and small dresser for his clothes. By the time he outgrew his crib, they should be back on their feet and looking for a new home. It was perfect.

She asked Mr. O'Shaunessy if she could take some pictures to show her husband and get his approval. She had agreed not to do anything else without their joint approval. He was happy to give her a few days to decide and Amy took pictures of both inside and outside.

Christopher was thrilled with the pictures and agreed it was perfect. While he loved his in-laws, he was happy to be home alone with his little family. Amy called Mr. O'Shaunessy and told him they would take it. She went through their furniture and kept only what would fit in the garages. The rest she sold and used the money to purchase what else they would need and groceries to stock the kitchen. The next weekend, the families helped her move the little bit of their stuff they were bringing with them. That Saturday night, Amy and the baby spent their first night in the cottage.

Soon, it was time for Christopher to come home. His parents went to pick him up and brought him straight to the little cottage.

They let him off at the front door and didn't come inside. They wanted the reunion to be between the three of them alone.

Amy opened the door and flew into Christopher's arms. They hugged and kissed as if they couldn't bear to let go. Finally, there was a cry behind them and they separated with a laugh.

"I'm sure this won't be the only time he gets the last word in, do you?" And he turned to take his son in his arms, the first time as a free man. It struck him that even with all the things that had taken place, he truly was blessed. He had a loving wife, a beautiful son, and a place to call home. They took the baby and went out into the garden. Passing through the kitchen, Christopher could smell all his favorite dishes cooking on the stove. There was even an apple pie sitting on the window sill.

It was difficult at first for the little family to get into a routine. Amy had been taking care of things and she reminded herself to let Christopher take over some of the responsibilities. Within a month, they had settled into life as a family, Christopher had found a job at a local mechanic's shop and Amy continued to stay at home with the baby. The parents all came to visit each Sunday, with everyone contributing a dish for the meal.

As Christopher sat and looked at looked at everyone gathered around the living room, taking turns balancing food and baby on their laps, he smiled.

It was good to be home.

Jason

The 2000s

Jason rolled over and hit the snooze button for the second time. He found it harder and harder to get up for work. It wasn't that he didn't like his job, he did. It was something else, he just couldn't put his finger on it. He hopped in the shower, making it a little bit icy to wake himself up. He got dressed in the regulatory suit and tie, grabbed his bag and ran out the door. Luckily, the elevator was going down and he was able to stop it on his floor. He nodded at the doorman, headed out and down the street at a brisk walk.

It was a hot beginning to the day and sweat already beaded on Jason's forehead and ran down his back. The sky was a beautiful shade of blue, at least the part you could see between the buildings.

He tried to be optimistic as he breathed in the exhaust fumes from the cabs rushing to take everyone to work. After all, this had been his dream since he was in college; get his master's degree from Harvard and get a job on Wall Street. He had allowed himself ten years at the most to achieve this and he'd done it. He was now a hedge fund analyst at one of the top five firms on Wall Street and was paid very well for that privilege.

He stopped at his favorite coffee shop, Perks of Manhattan, and grabbed his regular americano with a splash of cream and an extra shot of expresso. That jolt of caffeine should get his day started, at least he hoped so. He kept up his pace as he walked down Broadway to the financial district. He glanced at his watch, fifteen minutes, plenty of time. He slowed down and took in the sights as he walked hoping to calm his uneasiness. Why was he so restless lately? Wasn't he happy? He had a great job and a beautiful girlfriend. What more could he want? That was the problem, he didn't know.

He thought about Amber. He was lucky she even gave him the time of day. She was smart and beautiful. He had met her at a work function in the garment district. She was a model and had worked the show that night. He noticed her the minute she walked out, sleek auburn hair hanging straight to her waist and the greenest eyes he had ever seen. He couldn't take his eyes off her. Suddenly, as if she felt the weight of his stare, she turned and gave him a slight smile. That was it. He fell and fell hard. Within the week, he had her phone number and set up a first date.

He wined and dined her, showing her what dating him would be like. He pulled out all the stops. Amber soaked it up as if it was her due. Amber lived and breathed New York. She wanted to be seen in all the right places with all the right people. She insisted he escort her to all the 'in' parties. She took him shopping and updated his wardrobe to suit her tastes. Sometimes he found it exhausting keeping up with her energy. There were nights he just wanted to stay in and relax, but not her. She was go, go, go all the time. So, he went along with all of it, was glad to in fact, just to be with her. Who else could say he was dating the girl on the Times Square billboard?

Jason shook his head and sweat rolled into his eyes. He needed to stop daydreaming and get to work. At this snail's pace, he would be late. It was already eight and he still had a block to go.

As Jason entered his building, he heard a loud boom. He walked back out the door and looked around to see if he could tell what direction it had come from. Loud noises were not uncommon, but this one was louder than the usual. Not really able to see much from street level, Jason went up to his office. As he entered the foyer, people were rushing from desk to window and speaking in high, excited voices.

"What's going on? Why is everybody looking out the window?" Jason asked as he walked over to look out himself. To his horror, he saw fire and smoke coming out of one of the Twin Towers. "What? Do you see what I see? How in the world does something like that happen?"

Someone rushed to turn on the news and everyone gathered around the TV. The whole office stood in stunned silence as they listened to the announcer's stumble through the broadcast. As far as they could tell, a plane or something had hit one of the towers. Then as everyone watched, the unimaginable happened, a plane hit the other tower.

Jason looked around at his colleagues. Everyone was stunned. Some were crying. Others were frantically dialing on their phones. He was unsure what to do. He stared at the TV in disbelief. As if frozen to the floor, he just stood there with his mouth hanging open. A million thoughts ran through his mind. Were more bombs or planes coming? Would they hit more buildings? Who's behind this? Were we at war? Are they hitting other places? Is this all over the United States? What should he do? Should he try to help?

All these questions and yet he still stood there. He heard his coworkers talking all around him but he couldn't understand a word they said. He just stood there as everyone rushed around him. Finally, Mike, his buddy, came up and shook him by the arm.

"Come on, Jason. We're all getting out of here or at least going down to street level. Who knows if something will hit this place? Come on, we're taking the stairs just in case."

Jason fell in behind the others on the staircase. Walking down twenty floors was no easy task but it was better than being stuck in an elevator. The noise was insane as it echoed off the concrete walls. One older lady, terrified, had stopped on the tenth floor and sat unable to go on. Jason and Mike each grabbed her arms and half guided, half carried her down the stairs.

They burst through the stair door and onto the street. It was chaos. People were running around and crying. Traffic had stopped, people climbed out of the cabs. Everyone looked north at the towers and scanned the sky for more planes. Jason and Mike pushed their way through the crowd.

"What do we do, Jason?" Mike yelled.

"Maybe we should go see if we can help," Jason yelled back.

"Jason, you know the police and firemen are already there. What could we do that would help anyone? I'm getting as far away from this as I can. I'm going home." Mike turned right at the next cross street and ran off before Jason could stop him.

Jason stopped and stared at his friend's back as he ran off. He was surprised that Mike had not wanted to help out. He would never have thought of Mike as selfish. Well, maybe he was being self-preserving. No one really knows how they will react in a crisis. Jason knew he would not be able to live with himself if he didn't at least try to help. He started to run toward the towers, but it wasn't easy. Most of the crowd was running away from them and he had to push and elbow his way through.

He tried to cross over to Greenwich Street, but the wall of people pushed him back to the curb. It took him three tries to get across. Just as he placed one foot on the sidewalk, another wall of people began to push and pull at him. He lost his balance and began to fall. No one tried to catch him, if they were even aware, and he fell hard on the sidewalk concrete. His last view was of shoes as they jumped over his body, then nothing.

It was almost dark when Jason came to. At least he thought it was darkness. It took him a few minutes to realize the sun was high in the sky, he just couldn't see it plainly. There were clouds of dust everywhere, so heavy that he found it hard to breathe. Why was there so much dust? What had happened while he was knocked out?

He tried to stand, but a wave of dizziness hit him and he sat back down. He put his hand to his face and felt cuts and abrasions all over. His ribs were hurting too. Had people just stepped on him while he was lying there? What had happened to common decency? Had it gone out the window in the panic? Finally, Jason got to his feet and tried to walk toward the towers again, but the dust got thicker and heavier. He had to turn around after only a few yards.

"Might as well go home," he said to no one. "I can't be of any help to anyone in the shape I'm in." He turned to walk home. The sidewalks were empty now except for a few people walking around in a daze. He tried to stop them to ask what was going on, but they ignored him and kept stumbling along.

He arrived at his apartment and was surprised the doorman was nowhere to be found. He got on the elevator, grateful it was working. Turning the key, he stumbled into his living room, thankful to be back in what he hoped was relative safety. He went into the bathroom and cleaned himself up as best he could. He looked like he had been in a fight and lost. Grabbing a water, he sat down and turned on his TV. He watched in horror as the graphic scenes were played over and over. He couldn't believe it. The dust he had been choking on was from the collapse of both towers. So many people. Tears fell from his eyes at the thought of how many people he spoke to everyday had possibly lost their lives.

It was only two in the afternoon and so much had happened. He sat on his sofa the rest of the day and into the night, unable to take his eyes from the news. When exhaustion finally forced his body to sleep, he was jolted awake with the images of the day running through his dreams. He tried to call his friends and check on everyone except the lines were going in and out. He gave up and went back to the news. His brain was numb, but his heart was aching for all the people. The interviews were heart wrenching. So many lives lost and no one had any idea of the actual total that had been killed or injured. The Pentagon had been hit too, people injured there and the plane in Pennsylvania. The heroism of those people will never be forgotten, but what a horrific decision to have to make. Jason couldn't imagine what had been going through their minds as that plane went down.

Jason wondered who he would call if he had been in any of those situations today. His parents had passed away in a car accident three years ago and he had no sisters or brothers. He had tried to call Amber earlier, but had gotten her voicemail. She was out of town for a photo shoot so he knew she was safe, but he would just feel better if he could hear her voice. He thought about calling Mike, however he was still disappointed in the actions of his friend. He had believed they felt the same way about helping out when they could. Guess he was wrong.

He got a call the next day from his boss, not to check up on him, but to let him know the office had gotten some damage and would be closed for the foreseeable future.

He tried Amber later in the day and got her voicemail again. Now he was beginning to worry. It wasn't until the fourteenth that he got a call from her. She was mad that he was upset with her. She'd been working on set and was too tired to call. He knew she hated watching TV and she never paid attention to what people were talking about. They bored her. So why was he mad at her? He knew those things about her already, but they hadn't bothered him until now.

He tried to tell her what had happened, but all she cared about was how this would affect her career. He told her about getting nearly trampled, but she quickly turned the conversation back to her. Why had he never noticed how incredibly selfish and self-centered she was? Was he so enamored by her looks and status that he overlooked it? He had enjoyed her being seen on his arm, but was it worth putting up with this complete disregard for his thoughts and feelings? Did he really want to be with someone with so little regard for the suffering of other people?

He was glad she had to get off to go to a small after party. He couldn't stand one more minute listening to her constant chirping on about herself.

He turned the sound back up on the TV. More interviews with survivors. Their stories broke his heart. He watched nothing but the news for the next three days until he got word to report back to work. His heart sunk at the news. He felt like his life had changed and he was no longer eager to get back into that rat race.

Jason got up the next morning, put on his suit and tie, and headed out, but his heart wasn't in it. He looked at the blown-out windows at his coffee shop and he prayed everyone there was all right. He looked at all the other windows and doors boarded up and felt an intense sadness. How was he supposed to go on with life as usual when so much had changed? He had to watch where he stepped to avoid chunks of concrete that littered the sidewalk. He passed by where he had lain that day and felt a shiver run down his back. It could have been much worse.

The workday was filled with never ending meetings. Everyone was going to need to pitch in and work harder to get things back to normal. Jason wondered what normal was anymore. All his coworkers nodded as if what had happened was just a blip on their computer screen. Even Mike acted that way. Was something wrong with him that he couldn't just forget it and move on?

He walked slowly home that night. His mind filled with never ending questions of what ifs. What if a plane had hit their building instead? What if they hadn't helped that lady, would she have gotten trampled like he did? What if he had gone to a meeting at the towers that morning? What if, what if. He arrived home exhausted but no clear answers to his questions.

This had to be the longest week of his life. Rescue efforts were still ongoing with discouraging results. But his work went on without much change. He was finding it harder and harder to keep his mind on hedge funds and their importance. He knew his job was important but was finding it more difficult to convince himself it was important to him. Something had shifted and he was looking forward to the weekend to give it some serious thought.

Amber called him Saturday wanting him to escort her to an event in Connecticut that night. She didn't so much as ask him but expected him to do it. He realized he'd had enough of her selfish attitude and told her things just weren't working out between them. She huffed and puffed, told him he'd regret it, and hung up. He felt as if one of the weights he'd been carrying around had been lifted. What a relief! Now to figure out what else was bothering him and how to solve it.

Saturday night he reflected on his life and what he wanted. It had always been an Ivy League education and a high paying job, but now he wasn't quite sure. His job did not fill him with that sense of accomplishment it once had. He did not feel that he was doing anything to help the world around him by analyzing hedge funds. He wanted to do something different. He wanted to help people in some tangible way but he couldn't think of how.

Jason wouldn't admit it to anyone, but he no longer loved living in all the hustle and bustle of a big city. This past week, while he knew it was not the normal, he now hated the walk to work. He hated not seeing the sky except through the small cracks between each building. He hated how people walked, never making eye contact. He missed having meaningful conversations with people. When he weighed the pros and cons of his life, the cons far outweighed the pros. How he had changed this much in these last two weeks or had he been changing all along and this just solidified his feelings of unrest?

By Sunday night, Jason had given the apartment manager his notice. He had written his letter of resignation and emailed it to his boss. He walked through his home and decided to only take the necessities. He was looking for a simpler life. Perhaps he could find someone to take all his furnishings? Now where to go was the big question.

He had always heard of Southern hospitality and he sure could use some of that right now. He looked at places to rent in some of the smaller towns in Tennessee. He found one close enough to a big city if he needed it, but far enough away to still have some small-town charm. At least he hoped so. He looked at any ads that were described as being tucked away or remote. He had more than enough of apartment living. He was hoping for something small and out in the woods. As if by thinking, he had manifested it, an ad for a small remote cottage appeared in his search. It could even be rented furnished. It sounded perfect. Jason jotted down the number to call, wondering why there was no email listed. Noting it wasn't too late to call as they were an hour behind him, he tried the number. To his delight, it was answered on the first ring by an older sounding man with some kind of accent. He didn't think it was southern. He asked if the house was still available. Mr. O'Shaunessy, as the man introduced himself, assured him it was. After going over the rent, which Jason couldn't believe was true, they set on a time to move in.

Within a few weeks, Jason had packed up his clothes and anything else he thought he might need. The people taking over his apartment wanted his furniture so that fell right into place. He realized he would need a car, but to avoid finding a place to park it, he waited until the last minute to buy one. The day came when he was ready. Goodbye, New York. Tennessee here I come.

The trip south was a long one but pleasant, once he figured out which interstates to take. Thank goodness for GPS. The fear of leaving behind everything he had known overtook him at least once an hour but he forced it back with the excitement of this grand adventure. That's what he thought this was, a grand adventure. He was forging a new path to a new person.

He found the beauty of the leaves changing, a soothing balm to his nerves. The mountains of Pennsylvania and Virginia had the most colorful ones. He couldn't believe how beautiful they looked on the mountains. He hadn't even known there were such sights to see, having spent his life in big cities. Even the larger cities he had to drive through didn't have the big skyscrapers he had grown accustomed to. The sky was the bluest blue he had ever seen and you could see all of it. Colors appeared more brilliant without the smog and haze. The trip alone had made it all worth it.

When it started growing dark, he decided to stop for the night. He wanted to be well rested for the last of his trip and to be able to relax and enjoy it. He could barely sleep, he was so excited to see his new home. Home. He had never really thought of New York as home. It was so big and people seemed so disconnected. He supposed it was alright for others, but it just never seemed like a good fit for him. His soul longed for a quieter, more peaceful existence.

He grabbed breakfast at a quaint little diner. The waitress was so friendly and he ate more good food than he'd had in a month. Stuffed beyond words, he practically waddled to the car and resumed his journey. He thought the mountains he had seen before were beautiful, but they didn't compare to the mountains in East Tennessee. They had a blending of colors that he had not seen before. He took the extra time to get off the interstate and take some backroads and it was well worth it. He went through towns so small they only had a post office and one stoplight. He loved it. He felt the tenseness in his shoulders relax and the knot in his stomach was beginning to loosen. He rolled down the windows and breathed in the fresh mountain air. What a change.

He did have a moment of panic when he saw smoke coming out of several barns along the way. He pulled into the first store he came to and told them. He suffered a good laugh at his expense as they explained that the farmers were just 'firing' tobacco. First lesson of country living learned.

Driving through rush hour traffic in Nashville, Jason was glad this was his last big city to go through. About another hour and he should be right on time to meet up with Mr. O'Shaunessy. What an unusual man. He could only hope that the house was what he said it was.

Jason got lost a couple of times as it was growing darker and street signs were not well lit. He phoned Mr. O'Shaunessy, apologized for being late and got clearer directions. Turning around, he crawled along until he caught a glimpse of the small sign marking Dragonfly Lane. No wonder he missed it the first time. It was not a road but more of an overgrown path. He cautiously turned down it, driving very slowly as absolutely no moonlight came through that canopy of trees. After what seemed like a mile, the path opened up into a clearing bathed in moonlight. A small house, the smallest he had ever seen, was positioned in the middle of it.

A small, roundish man stood at the front door. He was wearing some kind of hat and carried a cane. He looked like he had stepped out of the nineteenth century. His face lit up with a smile as Jason exited his car.

"Well hello there! I hope you had a pleasant trip. I won't keep you long, just a quick show around and I'll pop right off."

Jason still couldn't make out his accent, but after his travels these past two days, he knew for a fact it wasn't southern. After showing Jason around the cottage and leaving the oversized key, Mr. O'Shaunessy was good to his word and left quickly.

It didn't take Jason long to unload the car. He sat everything inside the door. Unpacking could wait until tomorrow. Right now, he wanted to sit outside under that moon and listen to the quiet.

He settled himself in a chair and closed his eyes. Within seconds, he was aware of a cacophony of noises around him. He wasn't sure what they all were. He made out some frogs croaking nearby and the familiar sound of crickets. The rest he would just have to learn. The soothing sounds soon put him to sleep. He woke up hours later, slightly cold and covered with dew.

He went in to get a shower and found it so tiny that he had to stoop over to wash his hair. He unpacked his clothes and set up his computer. Realizing he hadn't eaten last night, he decided to go tour the town and pick up some groceries.

Driving down the lane in the daylight, he could appreciate the beauty of the trees linking their tops together. They were just changing colors and he liked the rustling sound of the dropping leaves under his tires. Something he had never experienced before.

Jason had soon toured the whole town. It had a post office, one bank, a few restaurants, and two stoplights. It was perfect. The grocery was an old fashioned Piggly Wiggly, but was fully updated and stocked on the inside. He took his time going up and down the aisles, picking out anything that looked interesting. He did stay away from the liver cheese, buttermilk, and hog jowl. Maybe later, when he was braver, but he doubted it.

He found it unusual, but nice, how friendly everyone was to him. All the people he passed in the aisles smiled at him, said hello, and asked how he was doing. He did get a lot of questions about where he was from. He guessed his accent gave him away. Even the bag boy was nice, he offered to carry his bags out to his car and refused the tip he offered him.

Returning home, he stocked his kitchen, made a sandwich, and headed back outside. Now he could see the small garden that surrounded the patio. He'd only had a house plant before and was anxious to try his hand at gardening. He suddenly realized he hadn't even thought of turning on his computer since he'd been here. That was certainly a change and a welcome one. He stretched out in the chair and took a nap, another thing he hadn't allowed himself to do in ages. This move had been the best decision of his life.

After a week of exploring and relaxing, Jason decided it was time to figure out what he wanted to do for a job. It definitely wasn't an analyst and he didn't want to commute to Nashville anyway. He'd had enough of traffic and crowds to last a lifetime. He broke down and turned on his computer for the first time since he got there. He began to look at jobs outside of his comfort zone. If he was going to change, he was going to change everything.

All the jobs he applied for were met with all kinds of questions. Why had he moved? Why didn't he want to continue in the field he had trained in? What was it like living in New York City? Was he anywhere near when the towers fell? Did he see them fall? It was all too much. He needed to give this job search a break. He had enough money saved to last awhile without worrying and the cost of living was much less here.

He found those questions were also bringing back the nightmares. He often wondered if he should see a professional, but he had always been good handling his own problems. Sitting in front of his computer one day, he was hit with an idea. What if he wrote about his nightmares? Other people had written about theirs, about their PTSD, and how it had felt to be there at that time. Perhaps that would help him, to get his thoughts down on paper. What could it hurt?

He opened up a blank document and stared at it. And stared. And stared. How does someone start something like that? He closed the computer down and went back outside. He'd start tomorrow.

The nightmares came with a vengeance that night. He woke up with sweat pouring down his face. He shook his head to clear it. Wait a minute, he reached over on the nightstand for a notepad. He had the perfect beginning for his book and he jotted it down quickly.

The next morning, he sat down at his computer and this time the words seemed to pour out. He started out with his life in New York, his relatively normal life until that morning. He wrote until the sky began to darken. He realized again that he'd skipped lunch and decided to try out one of the local restaurants instead of cooking.

When he opened the door to the diner, he was greeted with hellos and welcomes. What a difference. He was beginning to appreciate it more and more. It made him feel welcome and that was a wonderful feeling. He felt like people were becoming used to seeing him as a regular fixture in town. He was seated by the nicest waitress. Her name was Joyelle. She filled his drink with tea before he could say anything. He took one sip and made a face. When he asked for unsweet tea, she looked at him and said that was a sure tell he wasn't from the south. He explained he had not quite gotten a taste it for yet. Way too sweet. She laughed and he appreciated the way her eyes sparkled.

Again, that night, he dreamed. Was this the price he had to pay to heal? Then so be it.

He started a routine of writing every morning. Some days it came easily. Some days it was pure agony to get even one word onto the page. He kept at it and rewarded a good day by trying out another of the restaurants in town. It didn't take long to run through the three, so he would begin the rotation again. His favorite was the diner. He told himself that it was the variety they offered, not the twinkling blue eyes of Joyelle.

It took him two months to work up the courage to ask Joyelle out. But he wasn't sure what to do on a date here. They didn't have clubs or fancy restaurants. They had a theatre but it was playing a horror movie and he wasn't sure if that was good idea for a first date. He decided to just come right out and ask her what people did here for a date. She smiled shyly and said most went riding down the long, winding country roads. If the weather was warm enough, they had a picnic. Some rode down to the nearby lake and watched the boats. You could go into the next town if you wanted. They had more to do. He asked her what she would prefer and she said she loved riding through the countryside. He asked her then if she would consider going riding with him Sunday afternoon. To his delight, she said yes.

Jason washed and polished his car to get ready for his date. He dressed in jeans and a button-down shirt, nothing too fancy, but he felt he looked presentable. He drove to her house, thankful she didn't live too far out of town. He couldn't help but notice how cute she looked in her flowered dress and cowboy boots. He held the door open and she slid into the seat.

"You look very nice today," he said.

"Different from that uniform, right? You look very nice yourself," she replied.

"You give directions and I'll drive. You know these roads better than I do. We would probably wind up lost if you leave it up to me."

Joyelle started saying what road to turn on and Jason followed her lead. He soon realized that washing his car had been a waste of time, as some of the roads were dirt paths. But he didn't mind. Joyelle was so easy to talk to and he found himself telling her things he hadn't ever told anyone else. He told her about that day in New York and how it had made him feel. She just let him talk, not asking a lot of questions. It felt good to share his feelings with someone that seemed to care. He even told her about the nightmares and how he was journaling to help deal with them. She was glad he had found an outlet for what he had gone through. Before the date was over, he asked if she would like to read the first chapters. She accepted and seemed honored to have been asked.

Before they realized, it was growing dark and they turned around and headed back to her house. He apologized for talking so much, but she said she enjoyed every minute. She said she loved listening to him tell his stories. No one had ever told him that before and he was flattered.

When he dropped her off, he asked if he could see her again. She said she had Thursday off and it was supposed to be nice that day. She would pack a picnic and she would show him the lake that was nearby. He quickly agreed and they set a time to meet.

Between the writing and the dating, time was passing at a steady pace. He felt he knew his little town much better and was beginning to feel at home here. The nightmares were even getting fewer and further between. Life felt worth living again.

He still stayed in touch with some of his friends from New York. He and Mike were still friends, just not as close as they once were. It surprised him when Mike mentioned a publisher friend of his that might be interested in his 'journal'. Jason had just been writing to help him process the tragedy and he wasn't sure why anyone would be interested in reading it, let alone publish it. But Mike insisted, so he sent off what he had written so far, not expecting to hear back from it.

To his surprise, he got a phone call from an editor. She was extremely interested in the recount of his feelings during that time and would like to talk to him about possibly publishing it. Jason was skeptical, but after some research online, found that she and the publisher were actually well thought of and came highly recommended. Mike kept pushing him to go for it. Even Joyelle believed it could help other people who were going through the same thing. With their support, Jason arranged for a flight back to the city to meet with the publisher.

His stomach was in knots as he boarded the plane, he hated flying now. He put on his headphones and tried to concentrate on the movie. As they circled the airport, preparing to land, Jason couldn't help but notice how different the skyline looked now. It was incredible to think of how much everyone's life had changed since that fateful morning.

The publisher sent a limo to pick him up from the airport and he couldn't keep from laughing as he texted Joyelle to fill her in. He had left the city in a used Ford and was returning in a limo, he couldn't quite believe it.

He was wined and dined those three days and Jason was surprised at how little these things impressed him now. He longed for his return to his small town and his little cottage hid back in the woods. At the end of the visit, Jason had signed a contract to publish his journal and promote it. Life sure was taking a wild turn.

On his return to Nashville, he was anxious to see Joyelle and give her all the details.

"So sorry I couldn't afford a limo to pick you up, Mr. Freeman. But my little Nissan will have to do," she said and gave him a big kiss.

"You could pick me up in a buckboard wagon and I wouldn't care. Let's get out of here and get back home. I've missed you terribly."

Jason continued to write. He had two months to get his journal to the editor. He spent his days working out on the patio. Nights he spent with Joyelle when she wasn't working. After spending those three days in the city, he was extremely grateful for the peace and quiet afforded him here.

He felt truly blessed.

Soon, a whole year had passed and as September rolled around, Jason couldn't help but reflect on his life. Here he was with a book coming out in a few weeks and a fiancé that he loved with all his heart. He thought back to that day in New York when he felt like his life was over. It still turned his stomach to knots, but it was getting a little easier every time he talked about it. And he guessed he would be talking about it a lot for the next few months, as he had book tours scheduled in all the major cities.

He still hated flying, but it too was getting easier. He would just picture Joyelle waiting back at home for him and forget everything else. They had planned the wedding for the month after the book tour. Joyelle kept busy planning it all and he kept busy agreeing to it all. He wouldn't tell her, but he didn't care about the wedding itself. All he really cared, was that at the end of that day, she would be Mrs. Joyelle Freeman.

Jason shifted his shoulders in his suit jacket. He mentally prepared to talk about it all again. Different city, same talk. Everyone was fascinated with the tragedy. The only way he could get through it at all was remembering that half of the profits were going to the survivors. He did not feel right getting paid to talk about their heartache and not give something back in return. Joyelle had supported his decision and was proud of him for it.

After the wedding, they would return to the little cottage on Dragonfly Lane. Jason had thought about trying his hand at writing a suspense novel centered around Wall Street. He had some ideas and his publisher was anxious to hear them. It would be nice to put the tragedy behind him at least for a while. He knew it would always haunt him, but he had found a way to channel that fear and grief into something more positive and for that he was truly grateful.

Tilly

Late 2000s

Tilly drove slowly down Dragonfly Lane. How had it not changed in all these years? The trees still met in a green, leafy canopy and the road was just as it used to be, barely a path. There was still only the one house on Dragonfly Lane. She gasped at the sight of it. Ivy still grew along the house walls, effectively hiding it from the world and making it seem a part of the forest itself. It was still just a small red brick cottage with black shutters and a forest green door. Large paned windows opened out onto the yard that had little grass, but was full of clover and wildflowers. There was the small chimney still in the center of the red tiled roof.

It was as if time had stood still for the little cottage. She only wished she could say the same for her. Time had been good to her, she couldn't deny that. She had four children, ten grandchildren, and five great grandchildren with one more on the way. In that way she had been truly blessed.

The one thing that saddened her and to which she grieved to this day, was the loss of Sam. He had passed at the age of 83 from cancer. She had been with him, holding his hand, when he drew his last breath. They had shared a love that many didn't get a chance to find. It was truly a meeting of two hearts, two souls, and she was blessed to have had that time with him. But then, a million years would not have been enough for her.

One of the last things they discussed before he died, was what she should do once he was gone. He wanted her to move in with one of the kids, but she had disagreed. She didn't want to burden them. They had their own life to live and she wanted to give them the freedom to do what they wanted without having to worry about her. They had finally come to an agreement. She would move back into the little house on Dragonfly Lane if it was available and she was still able to care for herself.

When Sam passed, Tilly reached out to the owner of the little cottage. She was surprised to find that a Mr. O'Shaunessy still owned it. Surely it was his son or grandson, but she didn't ask. She was just relieved to find that it was still being rented and would be available the next month.

Her kids and grandkids all came and helped her go through the house. She let them take anything they wanted. All she cared about was her pictures and Sam's clothes. She liked to go stand among his clothes and smell his scent that still lingered on them. Her kids were not pleased with her decision to live alone, but that's exactly what she wanted to be, alone. Alone to be with her memories. That's all she really had left of her Sam.

When Tilly stopped the car, standing in front of the green door was a little man with a hat and cane. He looked just like she remembered. It couldn't be the same man, but funny how much he resembled him. Well, she's seen stranger things in her lifetime, just look at the man on the moon and computers. She couldn't explain them either.

After bringing in her luggage and lighting the gas logs for her, Mr. O'Shaunessy happily handed her the old-fashioned key. She decided to wait till tomorrow to unpack as the drive had worn her out. She found herself tired all the time now. She thought she was worn out from crying all the time. She never seemed to be able to stop, her grief was so great. Now that she was no longer in front of the kids, she could cry all she wanted.

She struggled to get the new sheets on the bed, then settled in front of the gas stove with a cup of tea. Now, she could let her memories find her here and settle in. She thought back to the day Sam had carried her over the threshold and they had begun their life together. She opened one of the smaller suitcases and pulled out the many letters and poems Sam had written her over the years. She carefully untied the frayed ribbon and opened the first of the yellowed pages. She ran her fingers slowly over the words as she read them out loud. Tears fell on the page and Tilly quickly wiped her eyes.

She fell asleep right there with the letters still in her lap. She woke to the sun streaming in the large windows, astonished that she had not even gone to bed. She moved stiffly as she placed the letters carefully on the table and gingerly got up from the chair. That was another thing about getting older. It took a lot longer to get anywhere. Moving slowly into the kitchen, she found the few things she had asked Mr. O'Shaunessy to stock for her. She fixed a piece of toast and a cup of coffee and went out to the patio. It was cooler than she had thought and was glad she had thrown on a sweater.

The birds were singing in the trees and the bees were flitting from flower to flower in the small garden. It was a beautiful morning and she felt peace more than happiness at her situation. Her intention was to live out her remaining days here until her time on earth was up. She counted the days until she would be with her beloved. It wasn't a maudlin thought for her. She was content with what she had accomplished in her life. She had received many blessings during her lifetime and she felt like her work here was coming to an end. She was pleased that she could spend what remained of it, here, with her memories.

Mr. O'Shaunessy agreed to stop in from time to time and check on her. He kept the garden tended and raked up the leaves when they began to fall. He also did her shopping for her. He really was a kind little man. Though she still couldn't quite make out his accent.

Tilly spent her days in the garden, reading her letters. Her nights in front of the gas stove, remembering bygone days. Her kids came to visit and would bring her favorite food and bouquets of flowers. She loved her time spent with them laughing and going over their favorite childhood memories. They were good kids and tried their best to cheer her up and she would be cheerful while they were there. But once the house grew quiet and she was alone, all the grief came crashing back.

She cried over the sad memories and the happy ones. She remembered the day Sam had come home from the war and how their life had begun anew. How he had cried when each child and grandchild had been born. How he would bring her flowers he would stop and pick by the side of the road.

She remembered how ill he had been there at the last and how she wished she could take the pain from him. How she wished it was her instead of him. She remembered how his hand had grown cold in hers. All her memories, bittersweet by the ending.

Days turned into months and Tilly wondered when she would be allowed to go to her Sam. Her grief was still as strong as ever, though she managed to hide it from her family. There were many nights where she cried herself to sleep. Many mornings she woke up with one of Sam's shirts clasped to her chest.

One morning she woke up with the memory of Sam coming to her in the night. He told her that it would not be much longer before they would be together. For her to be patient. The grief was all encompassing.

Tilly grew more tired as the days wore on. The only thing she managed to do was go back and forth from the living room to the garden. The days grew cooler and even that had to come to an end. She found herself once again falling asleep in front of the stove.

Her kids kept a constant check on her but she convinced them she was fine. They planned to all come see her that next weekend and check on her themselves. The thought of being cheerful for a whole weekend exhausted her.

She fell asleep that night after talking to each of them on the phone. She asked if they could make it another time as she was exhausted and everyone agreed to wait a few weeks and see how she felt. She was relieved. She snuggled up under a thick blanket and fell asleep.

She faintly heard the clock strike twelve and felt a presence beside her.

"Tilly, my love, it's time."

She opened her eyes and saw Sam beside her, not as he was at the end, but as he was the day they got married.

"Oh, Sam, I have missed you so much. Can I really go with you?"

"Yes, darling. Take my hand and we'll go together."

Tilly placed her hand in Sam's and stood up. She was no longer the old woman she had been.

Sam grasped her hand and began to walk out the green door that they had walked through so long ago.

Tilly and Sam were once again reunited, for all time.

Made in the USA
Columbia, SC
28 October 2024

45179259R00102